Black Fox Literary
MAGAZINE

Black Fox Literary Magazine is a print and online literary magazine published biannually.

Issue 21 Cover Art: *Ocean View* by Patti Sullivan

ISBN: 978-1-7336240-7-7

Editors' Note

The only way to kick this off is—Happy 10th Anniversary to *Black Fox Literary Magazine*! Congratulations to all of our contributors—those who are emerging in this our 21st issue, and those who've been with us from the beginning. We made it! Not even a pandemic could keep us from nurturing this labor of love. The struggle will not detour us!

Thank you to everyone who has submitted to our journal and to all of our readers and editors through the past decade. The depth of our gratitude is immeasurable. What began as a dream shared by a trio of graduate students has grown into a thriving member of the literary community.

We are committed to sharing your stories.

Thank you for your continued support and patience.

-The Editors
Racquel & Elizabeth

Meet the *BFLM* Staff:

Editor:

Racquel Henry is a Trinidadian writer, editor, and writing coach with an MFA from Fairleigh Dickinson University. She is also the Editor-in-Chief at *Voyage YA Journal* and owns the writing studio, Writer's Atelier, in Maitland, FL. Racquel has been a featured author, presenter, and moderator at writing conferences and MFA residencies across the US. She is the author of the novelette, *Holiday on Park, Letter to Santa*, and *The Writer's Atelier Little Book of Writing Affirmations*. Her fiction, poetry, and nonfiction have appeared in various literary magazines and anthologies. When she's not working, you can find her watching Hallmark Christmas movies.

Managing Editor:

Elizabeth Sheets is a writer and an editorial assistant for the *Journal of Proteome Research*. She earned a MA in Narrative Studies from Arizona State University. As a student, Elizabeth developed a passion for prison education. She has taught writing classes inside local prisons and corresponds with inmate writers about their creative work. Elizabeth enjoys a wide variety of different reading material. Some of her favorite authors are Elizabeth Gilbert, John Jakes, Roxane Gay, Stephen King, Anne Rice, Brandon Mull, Aimee Bender, and J.K. Rowling. Elizabeth's fiction, nonfiction, and poetry appear in *Kalliope – A Consortium of New Voices, Black Fox Literary Magazine, Mulberry Fork Review,* and *Apeiron Review*.

Founding Editors:

Pamela Harris lives in Greensboro, NC and spent seven years as a middle school counselor. Currently, she is an assistant professor in the Counselor Education Department at The University of North Carolina at Greensboro. When she's not molding the minds of future school counselors, she's writing contemporary YA fiction and middle grade. Some of her favorite authors are Ellen Hopkins, Courtney Summers, Roxane Gay, and Stephen King. You can also find her at the movie theaters every weekend or pretending to enjoy exercising. She received her MFA in creative writing from Fairleigh Dickinson University in 2012 and her PhD in Counselor Education at the College of William and Mary. Her debut novel, *When You Look Like Us* (HarperCollins), released in winter 2020.

Marquita "Quita" Hockaday lives in Williamsburg, VA. She is an adjunct professor who has never been able to shake her love of writing and reading. There is always, always a book near her. Marquita is currently enjoying writing young adult (historical and contemporary)—and most recently wrote her first middle grade novel with co-editor, Pam. Some of her favorite authors are Laurie Halse Anderson, Blake Nelson, Cormac McCarthy, and Joyce Carol Oates. Marquita graduated with an MFA in creative writing from Fairleigh Dickinson University in 2012, and completed her PhD at the College of William and Mary. She is represented by Savannah Brooks.

Contents:

Cover Art

Ocean View by Patti Sullivan

Wings, Tails
By Tria Wen
Winner of the 2021 Black Fox Writing Contest

When I was a few years old, I came down with a fever over 104 degrees. I remember flashes of it — being in that small, overheated body, hair matted to my temples by sweat, staring through the haze of a Vicks VapoRub humidifier. The other parts I remember were told and retold to me by Mama.

"When you tried to stand up, your legs crumpled beneath you," she'd say with sorrow, though she was talking to a healthy, grown version of me. Even the memory of her child in pain was hard to bear. She suffered during my sicknesses more than I did, hands a blur between soups, tinctures, compresses, too anxious to sleep. My recovery from that fever brought her such elation, it became part of the canon of our family stories.

"I was so worried we'd have to take you to the hospital. But then, I came into the room and you were sitting up, awake and alert. You told me you dreamed a flock of birds came and lifted you by your dress. They carried you with their beaks, and away you flew. When I took your temperature, the fever was gone."

In the world Mama raised us, ailments were treated with sleep, hot honey-ginger water, homeopathic remedies, and occasionally Chinese herbs or acupuncture. She loved retelling my bird dream, as proof of our connection to a spiritual world where a flock of birds could heal us, a testament to the fact that we possessed some magic hospitals didn't. She reminded me of it so often, I can still recall the birds clearly — the velvet of their beating wings above me, the firm grasp of so many sharp mouths on my clothes. Whatever magical world Mama believed in, I believed in it too.

—

The curtain that separates me from her is an indistinct shade, somewhere between green and nothing. I pause and draw breath before passing through, not knowing what she might look like in this environment: disembodied beeps, hurried shuffle of feet, cold fluorescent lights, antiseptic smells. It all must be squeezing her chest tight with anxiety, which is in turn squeezing me.

When I step through the curtain though, Mama is munching on ice chips like they're crunchy pork rinds. She's always happiest when eating, cheeks full like a little girl, nodding and making sounds of appreciation for the textures in her mouth. Her hair falls limp now on the shoulders of a hospital gown the same shade as the curtain, but other than that, she looks how she did at home this morning: emaciated and in discomfort, but present and bright-eyed, an injured sparrow regaining strength.

She lifts her hand and bobs her index finger up and down, a miniature wave that serves as both greeting and indication. She's pointing me out to the nurse, but raised me never to point, and to always make eye contact and use people's names.

"Luz, see that little one? That's my youngest." she gives me a wink, "We have to get me out of here soon, so I can go to her wedding." Her voice strains, but her tone is light, her eyes with their usual sparkle.

"Congratulations! When's the wedding?" Luz beams, as though we're chatting over brunch.

"October," I dip my head, not sure how to receive congratulations in a hospital room.

"Well, we're here to make you better, dear." Luz squeezes Mama's arm, and they smile at each other like old friends making plans.

I feel silly now for being worried. This is real life, not some tragic novel. It's Mama. She comes through every trial with a lesson and a metaphor to share. This may be the weakest state I've seen her in, but that's why this recovery will be particularly meaningful. It will be the reset that allows her to focus on all the projects she hasn't finished: the still-life watercolor series she began when I was in high school, charcoal portraits of her parents to match the ones she made of her grandparents, endless ideas for short stories, screenplays, novels and more. She hasn't broken the habit of splitting all of herself between the people she loves — her daughters, grandson, husband, relatives, many friends — leaving little for herself. But this was her wakeup call.

The call is in the form of a blockage in her colon that's been keeping her from having bowel movements for weeks. Her belly rises like a summer watermelon, protruding from her now seventy-eight-pound frame, body waning as her belly waxes. Looking at the swell under her sheet, I realize I do have one image in my mind of her in a hospital: a photo from when I was born, twenty-five years ago.

"This will be a rebirth," she says, as if seeing into my mind. "In a way, I am pregnant with myself." Her face lights up, pleased with the symbolism. I look at her belly, taut with toxins, and wonder what this next birth will bring.

She should've come in earlier, the doctors say. Bops had tried, but when it comes to health, Mama is not the kind of person who listens to outside input, even from her husband. She listens only to her body, and her body said they could fight the sickness at home. So Bops provided Mama with a constant stream of massages, cups of tea, hot water bottles — even at-home enemas.

"Bops and I are like treble and bass clef — connected and in harmony," Mama liked to say. They had the kind of unconditional relationship I was trying to build with my fiancé, hopefully minus the enemas. It's hard to believe she had almost been a runaway bride. My sisters and I laugh whenever we hear the story: the morning of our parents' wedding, she tried to jump out of the car on its way to church, but our grandfather pulled her back, the question "What are you doing?" loud in his wide eyes. She didn't know. All she knew was she was an artist, who still had things she wanted to make. But she loved the man waiting for her at the church's wooden chapel. She sat back down and buckled her seatbelt.

The doctors suggest placing a stent to clear the blockage, but want to see her more stable. They start her on liquids for strength, and morphine to help manage pain before next steps. As the medication drips in, I can see it dulling her senses and her presence. Soon she stops smiling. Stops saying our names. Making eye contact. She is asleep, I think, drained from the ordeal of the day. One of my sisters will stay with her overnight, we decide. The rest of us will try to rest and come back first thing in the morning.

The next day, she still seems far away, opening parched lips for ice chips through an oxygen mask. She's more morphine than Mama now, and I wish they'd hurry up with the procedure, so we can get back to making her stronger. I'll take time off work to care for her. We'll go to Hong Kong next month so she can see the best Chinese doctors and get her mother-of-the-bride dress made. We'll set up her painting studio together.

At lunchtime, we're all poking at something soupy in the cafeteria when we get a call to go back to her room. She's waking up — finally! We surround her, my fiancé hanging slightly back to give Mama's three daughters and husband space to each extend a reassuring hand, two of us on each side. I lean in, eager to hear her voice. The oxygen mask still obscures most of her face, but she opens her eyes and seems to see us clearly for the first time since yesterday. We look at her encouragingly — *Hi Mama! Yes, we're here! Everything's going to be okay!*

I cling to that eye contact in my memory because a moment after, I feel it: I feel her soul rush from her body. I'm holding her hand as the change sweeps through, a strong wind, a flock of birds pulling her away. Within seconds it leaves me in pieces. I hear my voice start to wail, crying in a way I've only been allowed to as a child in my mother's arms. I feel my body collapse into the collective body of my family, each of us bracing against one another in shock.

My spirit jolts and wriggles away from the wreckage, chasing Mama's quickly departing soul, grabbing ahold of the tail end and beginning a journey I won't be able to make sense of for years. When my waking self walks forward down the aisle, my spirit self will be whipping backwards through the curtains of time, still clinging to the tail of Mama's soul. After losing her, I will begin to look at her life not only in terms of us — our mother, Bops' wife — but in terms of her: a woman who wanted more time. When I begin the motions of creating my own family, behind my movements I'll be examining every crossroad, every decision, every lesson Mama taught me. When my marriage begins to crumble, I'll be flipping through the pages of her life to understand what could have gone differently.

Back, back, back. I will go back to August 26, 1972.

Mama will be sitting between her parents in the backseat of a car, slim body buttoned into a long white dress. Her breath will start to tighten as the enormity of the day looms before her. Stopped at a light on a steep San Francisco hill, she'll look up at the sun-drenched day and ask her parents to roll down the windows.

The air will smell of eucalyptus and hints of nearby saltwater. The sky will look to her like an open invitation — a welcome wideness above her narrowing path. A free bird of a spirit, she'll think to fly away into the big blue open, her white lace wedding dress fluttering behind her.

When she dives for the door handle, her father will try to pull her back, but she'll be out of the car, running, breathing, heart beating, beating. I'll find her there, on a wide street in the clear bright sun. She will know me, somehow. I will hold her hand again. Together we'll go looking for the life she didn't get to finish, the one I haven't yet started.

Another Fucking Nature Poem Pondering the Reason for Existence
By Gabrielle "Rie" Lee

I don't know how to label
this kind of pain. It's not
the dark, endless abyss of space
constricting my airway
like I'm used to. In those
moments I don't mind

if an eighteen-wheeler were to paint
my insides along the curb in front of my
house, my organs stuck
to the asphalt
like moist confetti.

Instead, I feel like the golden poppies
outside my window—stuck in the ground
between uneven pieces of desert-dry
wood chips rooted
in that spot
despite reaching
desperately
across the earth
to climb

out. Forced to do nothing
but watch the world and grow
at the gardener's mercy.

The pattern is the same every day:

      Wake up.
          Get older.
              Sleep.

In my waking hours
I reach my leaves across
the lawn in hopes that I'll find
some goal that leads to some prize
at the end if I've won. My leaves thirst

in the sun, dwindling yellow
in their exhaustion
and I know the gardener will cut

off my ends soon. But I persist in my quest
to find my goal as the street is quiet,
as the ants go about their burrowing business,
wishing I had a purpose like theirs—
        collecting resources for the survival
        of the species—
then withering as I realize I do.

T.H.A.W.*

By JC Reilly

Where, in the dark of a solemn heart,
can a crust of solace find its anchor,
or tether itself like tug to tanker,
as through a narrows that it will chart?
Some might say, when things fall apart,
that years will ease all pain and rancor,
that you might even come to thank her
or him you loved, for this melancholy part

of time. Not here, of course—too frail
and thick stands the space between cells,
that crushes hope to sediment—
and yet, that intrepid sliver, solace—pale,
glistening as nacre inside a shell—
will lodge unnoticed till its ascent.

*Time heals all wounds

Selected Poems by Lytey Kay

Nursery for Adults

When we're not in our pots or being watered, we sit,
a bench under dark netting. We all grow very close, smell
each other's dirt when it rains. Sometimes we absorb
the overflows of our neighbors, our roots sucking
on sitting moisture. We all agree that dew tastes the best,
which we learned from pollinators. They whisper as they sip
that it tastes like a cracked honeysuckle stalk, full of sugar
crystals and the temperature of spit. In the mornings when
I drink it, I think this is the closest thing to what we used
to call kissing. Some say all our rest, all this sitting is just
a machine for memory. That when we go into what we used
to call sleeping, we breath so long and deep it creates a fog
around us. That within the fog a stream of images unravel.
One time this made me cry. There danced the moment I held

my blind matriarch's hand in mine, felt the softness

of her knowing. Of the farm, the chicken's neck,
the kitchen sink, of the bare bottoms of her children.
Her veins were blanketed in what looked and smelt of ripe
mango and I was in awe at how skin returns to such softness.
When those that lived close to me tried to drink my tears
they all got sick and now there is a rule to never drink

another's tears. However, there is a rumor that if you

drink your own, you might not need to be watered anymore,
that maybe you can leave. And when we speak of this,
we just fall asleep and ask for more water when we wake.

A Vase for Panic, A Place for Panic, Space for Panic

Sitting is hard without hugging my knees,
but my fingers have started a consistent burning,
a coal buried in my back and glowing— ashing
into my ends. I do not nurture panic anymore,
well, it's been so long since I've felt it,
how an isolated burn can inflame a body, how
the day old sting of a jalapeño pepper becomes
an aneurysm. I call my mom, I have not talked to her
that day. S*hould I die mom, I want to hear
your voice.* [The word die makes me panic now,
consuming through the screen. Silly me.] I dreamt
of a mountain goat last night, it's curiosity in my bad
judgement, my trying shove of shoulders. He was real
close to my face and I could feel his lukewarm breathe.
I could see the shape of a mouth with no lips, could
imagine the texture of his grey pink gums before
they wrapped around my arm. He did not press hard
before he realized, I am not the food he likes. All the bad
things are coming out of me because I stopped eating
things like him. If I had any say in this, willing of something
by the name of god, I would graze the fields with him, but
today
I cannot write graze without subconsciously typing grave
instead.
I swore the other night I saw the grim reaper hanging
from my closet door. I watched *All Eyes On Me* and pondered
what could those moments feel like, right before it ends?
Do you know, on some level, can you feel it, am I feeling it
now?
Perhaps, I do still water a rose from the petals,

it's thorny stems on display as I eat.

This was supposed to be a happy poem
By Princess Berry

Golden rope,

always ready to hang the birds.

The beach sand, green.

Can waves be dry?

The grasses creased,

The branches, just bones.

Write a timeline of the speckled constellations,

But the sky's a blur.

Loneliness can walk.

(Alonetogether)

Lonely, you smile,

And choked in the end.

Name your questions:

"Is the world alone too?"

Just Sing.

Sing to photos,

Just Wish, (gently), to be the high,

you used to be.

Maybe,

We'll like smiling again.

Maybe,

You cannot be wrapped in the dead for too long.

He Never Brought Her Flowers
by RC Neighbors

It took a death to get Eric back to Oklahoma, to leave his work at the hospital in San Francisco, and head back to his hometown of Okay. By the time his cab from the Tulsa airport pulled into his parent's drive, Eric had nodded off against the window. "This the place?" the cabby asked.

Eric blinked at his boyhood home through the windshield. It spread out behind a circle drive, two stories, Corinthian columns in the front, fake shutters by the windows. It sat in the middle of an open field, and in the back, bluestem grass—now gold-colored for the autumn—grew against the fence line, high as a person's chest. It was one of the largest homes in the county, and his father Gene had paid for it through a life spent building the top construction company in the area.

After Eric grabbed his bag and paid for the cab, his brother Seth met him at the front door. "Hey."

"Hey." Eric stared at his brother. Seth's hair was long and disheveled under a maroon OU cap, and he hadn't shaved in a few days. He tugged at a stained, white t-shirt that was at least a size too big for him, like he was uncomfortable in his skin, was worried about his stomach pressing against the fabric. Eric wore his most expensive suit for the trip, a dark grey three-piece, and as the two brothers eyed each other, Eric felt overdressed.

"You haven't changed a bit."

"What's that supposed to mean?" Seth asked, a sour expression on his face.

"Um, nothing," Eric said. "Nothing." He took a step toward his brother, considered raising his arms for a hug, but he thought better of it.

Seth seemed abnormally interested in a crack on the porch. He kicked at it with the toe of his sneaker.

Before they could break the silence, their sixty-year-old mother Rita shoved her way in front of Seth. She wore a tight, black dress that showed a lot of her large breasts—anniversary gifts from Eric's father. Tits like a car wreck, Gene always said. Even if you don't want to look, you can't turn away. Rita pressed them against Eric as she squeezed him hard. "My boy is home," Rita said. "My baby boy."

"It's good to see you, Mom." Eric accepted the hug and kept a hand on her shoulder when they separated. "How have you been holding up?"

She explained that she was doing as well as could be expected. She was there when it happened, after all, heard his last breath croak out, so incredibly long, felt the ribs pop and crack when she tried and failed at CPR, ignoring the order not to resuscitate. The last few years had been hard for all of them, too, she said. Sponge baths. Unexplained fits of anger. And the incontinence. "That means he shit himself," she explained. "Oh, but you know that! My boy, the doctor."

"Um, yeah," Eric said and nodded. "That's common in the later stages of Alzheimer's."

"My boy, the doctor, so smart," she said. "And so nicely dressed, too." She looked from Eric to Seth, who stood silently behind her. "Seth, honey, look how nice your brother's suit is."

Seth disappeared into the house without answering.

Rita told Eric not to mind his brother. Seth was having trouble dealing with the loss of their father. After another hug, she led Eric into the house and down the hallway. In the living room the walls were covered with a big screen television and the mounted heads and bodies of dead animals of all shapes and sizes—fish and ducks, raccoons and rabbits, a deer and wolf and moose. Even a bear and a mountain lion stood in opposite corners of the room. But no elk. Eric remembered that Gene had always wanted an elk. There was a recliner next to the bear and a couch by the cougar and folding chairs spread throughout, all full of people—neighbors and aunts and uncles and cousins.

Rita pulled Eric around the room and introduced him—her son, the doctor—to all of these people he hadn't seen or spoken to in years. Eric accepted their pleasantries and their clichéd condolences with as much sincerity as he could muster. Eventually his mother dragged him to the kitchen where the marble counter of the mini-bar was covered with a hodgepodge of meats and vegetables and casseroles. Behind the bar, Eric's sister Allie helped people with the food, handing them Styrofoam plates and plastic cups. She was short, just over five feet, wore a pantsuit, and had dark bangs that hung over her forehead. She seemed very adult, Eric thought, with a new seriousness, doing her part to help during their mother's grief. At thirty, it was about time she looked her age, instead of the fresh-faced little girl she had always seemed.

When she saw him, she dropped the cups, ran to him, and swallowed him in a hug. She smiled up at him, and Eric could see that the little girl was still there, just under the surface, of the years or the grief or maybe both. "I'm glad you're here, bro."

"Me, too," Eric heard himself say, though his face didn't quite match the sentiment.

Allie waved behind her to a pudgy woman with close-cropped hair, and the woman walked over.

"You remember Allison's roommate, Melissa, don't you, Eric?" Rita asked. Eric glanced sidelong at their mother.

"Of course," Eric said. He shook Melissa's hand. "I'm surprised you've put up with her for this long."

"It surprises me sometimes, too," Melissa said and smirked at Allie.

As the conversation continued, Eric watched his mother's eyes gravitate toward the front door, to an overweight minister in a cheap, ill-fitting suit who had walked in. He held another casserole. Rita excused herself and walked over to him. When she had left, Allie elbowed Eric in the side. "I should get back to the visitors." She gave him that smile again. "But it *is* good to see you. We'll talk later."

Eric nodded and watched them go back to playing hosts to all the guests. He grabbed a beer from the fridge and roamed through the kitchen and living room, watching the people, overhearing their conversations. Every few minutes bouts of nervous laughter erupted from one of the groups, an old man's death apparently a humorous affair. Several times people he didn't recognize stopped him to tell some story or other he had never heard about his father. Like the time Gene went hunting, and an old boar surprised him and gored the hell out of his ass cheek. He went to the ER and needed thirty stitches, but that boar ended up on his wall. Gene always joked about expecting dinner first the next time. And maybe a movie. "Dinner first," the neighbor repeated and slapped his own knee.

Another told Eric of the time when Gene was younger and out on a job site, and someone dared him to glue his fingers together. And he did. They called him "Flipper" for a long time after that, even sang the TV show theme song on occasion. Still another told of the time Gene got so drunk that he decided to walk home along the train tracks, fell asleep there, and then awoke the next morning as a locomotive roared above him. He was lucky nothing hung across the track. As Eric discovered, the stories were always funny, about stupid things Gene had done or crazy things that had happened to him, and Eric smiled pleasantly and laughed at the appropriate times.

Eventually, Seth came into the living room, looking even more agitated than before. He leaned against the wall by the bear. Eric wandered over to him. "Where have you been?"

"On the phone."

Eric wanted to ask with whom, but that felt like prying. Besides, if Seth had wanted to say, he would have mentioned it. "So where's Kayla? She must be, what, six, seven, now?" He leaned against the wall on the opposite side of the bear, trying his best to look aloof.

"Nine," Seth said, running his fingers along the bear's claws. "She's nine and with her mother and is not coming," he grumbled. "She barely knew him anyway."

"Still having trouble with Karen?"

"Kristen," Seth said. "She's such a bitch. Hardly lets her spend time with me. I have rights."

"The way to treat women is to always act like what they ain't got," Eric said half-heartedly. He meant it as a joke, an attempt to lighten the mood, though even he didn't think it funny.

"You don't have to quote him," Seth said. "But you are a dick." He turned his back toward Eric, then walked in the direction of the kitchen. Eric shrugged and let him go. He directed his attention back towards the quiet conversations of the guests. Nearby Rita had finished discussing the funeral with the minister and started talking about how she was doing.

"That means he shit himself," Eric heard her say. The minister grinned.

***

The next day the funeral was uneventful. The church's sanctuary was big and typical—a stage, a center aisle, and two rows of pews, all in shades of red. The family sat on the front pew, Allie with her arm around their mother. Flowers of every color and shape covered the stage and surrounded the coffin.

Rita had picked out each bouquet herself, Allie informed Eric later; Rita had insisted on it.

Most of the town showed up to see off one of the wealthiest men among them. Eric wasn't sure why—if out of affection, curiosity, or a sense of vindication, the knowledge that Gene was like the rest of them after all, headed toward the same end, and that they, in fact, had beat him by sticking around longer.

The large minister in the cheap suit spoke for about twenty minutes. The service held little mention of Jesus or salvation, heaven or hell, or religion of any kind really. For as long as Eric could remember, his family had never attended church, and the minister's focus on Gene's life, no matter how one-sided, seemed appropriate. Eric wondered if his mother had asked the minister for a service like this. Either way, Eric appreciated it. The minister ended his speech by talking about how Gene loved life so much he lived over ten years after his diagnosis. Rita and Allie were the only people in the sanctuary that needed use of the complimentary tissues.

***

After the funeral that night they were alone in the house with the casseroles. The neighbors and cousins were gone, having done their duty. Those that remained sat in the living room, still in their funeral attire—Rita in her recliner and Allie, Melissa, and Eric on the couch under the moose head. Seth grazed on the leftovers in the kitchen. They caught up about the goings-on over the last few years. Rita's life was consumed with caring for Gene. Allie had finished her counseling degree and started work at a mental health clinic in Muskogee. Melissa was still in grad school. She wanted to be a speech pathologist.

Eventually, Rita said she needed a drink and fixed herself a Bloody Mary at the mini-bar, heavy on the Mary. She took the liberty of making everyone else rum and Cokes. As the evening went on, they refilled their glasses, and Allie and Rita began telling stories about Gene. Allie told about how over the last couple years, as the Alzheimer's got worse, he had been consumed with Barack Obama, going on and on and on about how the President was a fascist and a socialist and the antichrist and how he needed to be run over with a car. Rita laughed about when their father walked in on Eric, who was a toddler at the time, using Gene's new toothbrush to scratch his little bottom, right down the center. Gene had been so angry, but he couldn't scold Eric without laughing. "It's itchy," Eric had said, in his little toddler voice.

"There's nothing like that minty fresh feeling," Melissa said. "I hope that was the first time you did it, Eric, and not just the first time he noticed."

Everybody laughed even harder. As they continued to drink, their laughter grew louder and their stories more outrageous. So outrageous Eric began to think some of them were completely made up. He noticed, though, that Seth hadn't been laughing or even acknowledging the stories. He only leaned against the doorjamb, between the kitchen and living room, with his arms crossed.

Eventually, Rita and Allie asked Eric to share a memory, and after some prodding, he mentioned how embarrassed Allie had been the time Gene took her to Sea World and, after running out of underwear, washed his dirty pairs in the hotel sink and then dried them by hanging them out the car window.

"There were skidmarks," Allie said and crossed her arms in mock embarrassment. The whole room—besides Seth—roared with laughter that made it hard to breathe, and tears began to slide down their cheeks.

"He never brought me flowers," Rita said. Her face had grown lax, turned suddenly serious, and their laughter stopped just as suddenly. They stared at her, no one speaking, for several tense seconds. Rita grunted to herself, almost a chuckle. "He never brought me flowers, so one day I just said, 'Well, if you're not going to do it, then I'll do it myself.' And I went to the flower shop and ordered the biggest, most expensive bouquet they had. I still have the petals. I dried them and put them in a jar."

The silence lingered. There it was, thought Eric. The thing they had been avoiding over the last two days: his father was an asshole, and no matter how many funny stories were told, that fact would never go away. Nothing could change that.

For a long time, no one moved or said anything or even seemed to breathe. Eventually, Allie joined Rita on the recliner and held her hand.

"I miss him so much already," Rita said finally and cried onto Allie's shoulder. In disgust, Seth swore under his breath and left the room. They heard the front door slam and a car peel away.

"Go after him, Eric," Rita muttered. "He doesn't need to deal with this alone." Eric placed a hand on his mother's shoulder, nodded, and left.

***

Allie had told Eric to look for Seth at his trailer, but when he wasn't there, Eric tried the place where he worked. Eric pulled one of his mother's cars into a gravel lot off of Main Street. The building in front of him was covered in aluminum siding, and on the front of it, letters read, "Bob and Janet's Child Care and Storage." Multi-colored playground equipment—a slide, a sandbox, some monkey bars—stood in front of the building, and storage units spread out behind it. It was dark, and the lot was only illuminated by a single lamppost standing over the storage units. In front of one, Eric saw another of his parent's cars, so he got out and walked toward it.

Inside the open unit Seth stood in front of a canvas, splattering paint on it with his fingers and a brush, paint smeared all over his hands and face and shirt. Surrounding him were several other easels holding other paintings— landscapes and still lifes and portraits. "These are good," Eric said. "I didn't know you still painted."

"How would you?" Seth didn't turn around.

"Listen, if you've got a problem with me, then just say it."

"Five years," Seth said. He threw down his brush, turned toward Eric, and pushed him, smearing red paint all over his dress shirt. "Five years is my problem with you. Gene got sick a decade ago, and you left. You hardly ever called. Didn't answer your phone. Stopped coming in for holidays. We've barely heard from you and haven't even seen your face in five years. You left us to take care of him by ourselves."

Eric pushed him back. "Us? Don't you mean Allie and mom?"

Seth grabbed him in a headlock, and the two tumbled into the storage unit, along the smooth concrete, knocking over easels and buckets of paint. They grabbed and pulled, trying for holds, wrestling the way they fought as boys, too afraid to throw punches, too afraid of what a blow to the face meant. Within a couple of minutes, they were both lying on the concrete, apart from one another, winded and covered in paint.

"We're not as young as we used to be," Eric said.

"That's the first sensible thing you've said since you got here."

"Can you take it easy?"

"It's just this whole mess," Seth said, making a sweeping motion with his arm. "Everything. Dad was a jackass. A jerk to mom. Was quick with the belt if we stepped out of line. And everyone is acting like he was some sort of saint."

"He tried, you know. After the diagnosis, he made an effort. That's why he and Allie got along."

"Too little, too late," Seth said. "He had already cut me off by then. I didn't need his charity."

"Surely, you remember something good about him, don't you?"

"Well..." Seth stared at the aluminum ceiling and lit a cigarette. After exhaling a cloud of smoke, he told Eric about one time he remembered. Seth had been about eight or so, and Eric thirteen. They were wearing ties and button-down shirts. He didn't know where they'd been, but Gene took them out to the field behind their house for some reason. Seth couldn't even remember why. The boys marched behind their father through the grass, its tips almost as tall as they were, and suddenly Gene was gone. "You're it," he yelled, and they began a game of hide-and-seek, crouched in the high grass. They played until their socks were covered with burs and their knees with mud. Rita had been so mad they had ruined their nice clothes, but their father had only shrugged.

"He was still a jerk, though," Seth said. "You didn't want to stay."

Eric had been near graduation at OU Medical when his father got the preliminary diagnosis. Eric knew how hard it would be on everyone. The full-time care Gene would eventually need. And Eric ran.

"I'm sorry," he said.

They were silent for a long time. When Eric couldn't bear it any longer, he pointed to the storage units around them and asked, "So you work at a day care. You like kids now?"

"Can't stand them. I'm storage manager." Seth laughed but couldn't keep it up. "Kayla gets to come here for free," he added. "So, I at least get to see her most days."

Seth smiled wistfully for a moment, but it soon faded. "You know," he said. "Over the last few months dad would have these crying spells. He'd cry for over an hour at a time, mumbling about how his mom died and how his dad died, as if it happened that day and they hadn't been in the ground for almost thirty years." Seth cleared his throat and wiped some paint from his cheek. "Do you think we'll ever feel that way about him?"

"I don't know."

***

When they came home, Seth walked around back to have another smoke. Eric went inside and found Allie under the moose head in the living room. She had fallen asleep—or passed out—on the armrest of the couch, snuggled up with one of their father's sweaters. On the opposite side of the couch sat Melissa, her eyes wide and staring at him. Rita was shaking her ass in Melissa's face.

"I've been told I have a nice caboose," Rita said. "What do you think? Do you like it?"

Help me, Melissa mouthed to him.

"Mom, I think you've had enough," Eric said. "It's time for bed." He took her arm and helped her stand.

"You've been painting," she said, poking his shirt. She leaned against his side, and he led her out of the living room and down the hallway. In the hall, pictures lined the walls, an entire lifetime in blacks and whites and colors—babies and school photos, birthdays and weddings and reunions. They walked past the years, and Rita began to sing various songs that always turned into "Rhinestone Cowboy."

"How does that go?" she said. "Everything that glitters is not gold...like a rhinestone cowboy!"

Eric was too focused on the pictures to help her with the lyrics. He watched as he and his family aged, as he and his father grew apart, until finally Eric and his mother reached the end.

Inside the bedroom someone, probably Allie, had placed all the floral arrangements from the funeral. Eric helped his mother, still in her dress, to the bed and under the covers. He sat next to her and pulled the blankets up to her chin. On the nightstand stood the glass jar of wilted rose petals she had mentioned before, a reminder of who his father really was.

"He loved me," she mumbled in a half-sleep, pleading, as if trying to convince herself. "He did."

Eric started to go, but before he could leave the bed, Rita gripped his arm, her nails indenting the flesh of his wrist. She lifted her head from the pillow, and her eyes focused on his face in the dark. "He told me before the end," she said. "Not in words so much, but I know. I was giving him a bath, and as I brushed the washrag against his cheek, he touched my face. He looked at me, his eyes so clear I knew he was himself again, that he knew me, like the fog that kept him from us had cleared, just for a second. He said my name. That was all, and then he stared at the light reflecting from the faucet. You see, I know he loved me," she said. "I know."

"I know, too, Mom," Eric said, but her head was on the pillow again.

Eyes closed, she raised her hand to grope along the nightstand, searching for something. "Flowers," she muttered.

Eric handed her the jar of wilted petals, which she clutched to her chest. He grimaced, then slowly caressed her cheek with the backs of his fingers—like he pictured his father doing, nude and emaciated, waist-deep in a tub of soapy water, during a single moment of clarity.

***

Eric met Seth on the deck behind the house. He leaned his forearms against the railing next to his brother, and stared up at the night sky, the stars shining so brightly without the lights of the city to hinder them. Orion seemed to glow the brightest in his never-ending struggle with Scorpio.

"How is she?" Seth asked. He lit another cigarette, momentarily illuminating his rough face, and took in a deep draw.

"She'll be okay."

"He did a real number on her, didn't he?" Seth said. "The bastard."

Eric gazed past the fence, toward the bluestem grass waving in a cool breeze. He knew it was a gold color, like ripe wheat, but it looked pale blue in the moonlight. "No," Eric said finally, meeting his brother's eyes. "He was just a man."

From the glow of the cigarette, Eric could see his brother scowl, as if he was going to argue, but Seth only nodded. Eric stared past the fence again, at the bluestem that swayed in the darkness, and he felt the overwhelming need to run his hands over its tips, tromp through the brush. Without thinking, he jumped over the railing and onto the grass below and began to walk and then sprint to the fence line.

"What are you doing?" Seth asked and snuffed out his cigarette on the rail.

When Eric reached the fence, he spread apart the barbed wires, stepped between them, and vanished. "You're it," he said.

Seth swore and shook his head. Then he laughed, a small mirthless laugh, but a laugh still, and joined his brother in the high grass. They crawled through the field on all fours, each searching for the other, nearly blind in the darkness. They played like that together, for a long time, until burs covered their socks and the damp soaked through their knees.

concrete/rust/marrow
By Connor Beeman

my town is tired.

it is rust and gold.

it is indigo match
  and burnt out brick.

it is factories in amber.
  it is coal once long ago.

it is rubber and steel
  and burning water.

we built you once.
  we decay nonetheless.

my town is weary.

  it is ribs,
    stray dog,
      marrow sucked dry.

it is resilience.
  it is persistence.

  stubborn land, stubborn concrete,
the stubbornest people you'll ever meet.

it is opioid,
  it is overdose,
    it is abuse.

it is legacy,

it is history,
  it is endurance.

my town is an echo.
hear it.

decay. ending.
renewal. beginning.

Selected Poems By Derek Graf

Small Continuous Explosions

The trees give up their obsession
with the wind. Last night my lover
hit rock bottom, drove her truck
off the road into a cattle pasture.
I need to give up my obsession
with endings. Ants doused
in boric acid scatter along
the patio ledge, insane with death.
She wants to stop for a picnic
on the drive to rehab. She wants
a bottle of wine. Once she's gone,
dragged dead drunk into the arms
of orderlies, the days come on
like small, continuous explosions
inside me. The trees give up
their obsessions. They have to.
Last month the landscape
crews cut them all down.

Forms of Interiority

A body falls
          through the galaxies
inside an opal.

A body falls

on a mattress
after working all night
     at a construction site.

In this industrial forest,
     every cell of your body
dissipates into vapor.

We were united
     in our solitude, recalling
the dead eyes of horses
     smothered in toxins

at the rendering plant:
     looking away, staring back.

It was a Bull Fight
By Coleman Bomar

We were bull and matador both
Dripping red on many beat dead
Horses

We were the teethy crowd too
And their white knuckled
Noises

We were our walled arena
The ring was the world
The doors were so quiet
And hard to find

Paper Birch
By Letizia Mariani

On bark, the eyes of hundreds,
stacked like studded beads, see nothing—
rather, see somersaults of winter leaves,
the gutter's drool, the swinging
of the limp fingers of trees.
How much swaying they hold in their pupils
when they stare intent at the rising
and dying of time with enough peepers
to capture a swallow, but no mouth to say it.
Think of the birds that have grasped
the crooked limbs of birches. They combat
the loneliness of flight with botanical repose.
Think of the fledglings born under the brows
of trees; how they open their beaks in silence
and gape in mutual understanding.

Ebbing
by Marsha Lewis

Her pale Ovaltine in clean jars,
her ivory soap smell, little cracked
glasses along the ledge.
As she declined, I scrubbed
feathery, fuzz-green mildew
from the corners of the birdbath.

She grew softer as she ripened
into even quieter wisdom,
wrote tinier, tinier blue ink
words on thank-you cards.
The cardinal she knew to be
her husband visited the feeder.

She will lift a skillet in the kitchen
some afternoon before long
and stand still
while listening to a thing
unheard before, then put down
her heavy utensils, the old ways
of knowing, for the time
when they were needed
is past now.
It is tin, it rings in the ears,
a vague tinnitus.

And speaking from this
watery new place to the land-locked,
she sounds confused.
You'll hurry on in ramblings
to stun the hush, to fill it:
ask questions to keep her grounded,
place cups and calendars

near as reminders, but never mind:
the concrete cannot keep her here.

She has a rare silken quality
in her sinew, she goes
into the silvering spaces.

She lets go little bits of world daily.

Selected Poems by JB Hill

Dreaming of Loch Ness

I have a plan
to swim in the cold waters
of Loch Ness—
thousands of miles away.

Newfound records say
I have Scottish blood,
on the sunset and sunrise
sides of the family tree.

But the gene ties are
little threads, not lumbering ropes.
I don't know the ways
of Scottish women
or how they survive winters
and too much drink and the
lazy tide of this or that
trying to prop up institutions—
punishing ones that
outlasted long voyages
and deep time and bashings
left and right.

In my mind, they are all witches—
maybe sea witches or lake witches
or marsh witches.
I'm a river witch. I'll be fine.

I move with the current
on cold evenings under a full moon.
I swim in circles
watching Mexican free-tailed bats
fly low against the cliffside.

But Loch Ness is an icy portal,
filled with lore and pebbles,
light and misfortune,
lies and lingering songs.

Whatever rubs against
the pain tingling my skin
could be anything.

But, mostly, it is the shock of
foreign, mystical water—
underneath, home.

New

The tide has come and gone.
I live four hours from a beach,
but I know this is true. It is not new.
Neither is this poem. It has been written
a thousand trillion times plus one.

It was written by my 10th grade English teacher
one night after his girlfriend left him.
It was written by my older sister
in that hateful note she left me
before she moved out for good.
It was written by my neighbor
who keeps her house dark on Halloween
because she is scared of any sort of mask.
It was written in every
half-baked business plan that ever was.
It was written when I fell out of my old self
and into screaming love for the first time,
and then it was gone.

There was one grown up
without normal manners
who told me that everything that ever was
has already been
thought
written
sung
danced
painted
and cried over.

We twisted spoons together with our minds,
and drew pictures of heroic horses
and their unaffordable, fine black carriages
as though recalling a personal memory
and not something from last Sunday's movie
at the empty theater with sticky carpets.

I wrote the perfect title for the book
I will never write.
I sang the first spine-tingling chorus
to the song that will never been sung.
I stretched my tired, inflexible body
in a modern, screeching arch
when encountering harmless grass snakes
in the woods behind my house.
It was a dance always crouching
in the silent anxiety days drifting,
then rumbling.

For an hour, I grip
an orange and green glass marble
in a tight fist
convinced that my best idea
is trapped inside of it.

I fantasize that I might be able to
throw it so hard
it will pass through the drywall
without a scratch,
the universe reassembling itself
in honor of the only new thought
to come about in five thousand years.

Instead, I go outside.
It is cold under the Texas sky.
I find a scarf but keep my flip flops on.
The summer was a living hell,
I say out loud.
The wind pushes leaves into my face,
and I swat them away like fruit flies.
I should be grabbing them like
million-dollar bills or kisses.
I steer my head toward the stars
and know this has been done before.
I remember now
and bury the marble
next to the dead Peruvian Lemon tree
that died in last year's freak blizzard.

I survey the leaves at my feet,
gather them quickly
and release them to the wind like wishes.

Now, they are in my neighbor's yard.

Like Orange Essence and Vanilla
By Kris Faatz

Old Man Meacham seems more like a prison guard than a baker. The folks who line up at his shop every morning wonder how his boy Peter can stand working under his eye. It's Peter who makes the cinnamon buns that taste like that one perfect Christmas morning, and the meringues that laugh on the tongue. Even his "ordinary" breads aren't. While they fill the stomach, they wrap the heart around with strength and courage.

The lines of bakery customers stretch all the way down the street. None of those people knows that Peter's mom Lena taught him a potent secret: how to make joy, love, and memory into flavorings, just like orange essence and vanilla. They also don't know that Lena's magic holds her family together.

When she dies, too young, Meacham and Peter bury her and go back to work the next day. Meacham sits at the counter, his face like freezer-burn, while Peter works the ovens. Today, bread is just bread. The meringues are soft with loss. Everybody hears old Meacham scold Peter, but they don't hear what happens that night, after the bakery closes.

Hands with know-how can roll memory into pie crust. They can dust apples with cinnamon, sugar, and vanished joy.

When Peter takes this pie out of the oven, the scent warms the air like a loved voice.

Old Meacham accepts a slice from his son and closes his eyes to take a bite. When he opens them again, he's a boy, in love with a magical girl.

Selected Poems by Laurel Benjamin

Detained

all I could do, hands in pockets
bare legs on a metal chair
cross my tender feet

the manager's office
really an employee break room

like the blooming between tracks
in a railroad yard, inevitable
I would end up here.

Nothing sandwiched between the questions
I had of my future and the striped shirt
embedded in the hippocampus

weight of greasy handcuffs
a singular flutter.

Revving of a reborn engine of tinted
windows, radio codes I had no key for
and the overhead light

a vague caw from the seat
legs chafed as I adjusted
and though I could not see them

music of sharp stars
while the stray hair I could not reach
inserted itself under my glasses.

Never Forget

Never forget the terrible speed of birds
skirting on top of green water
how they dip, then come out

unscathed. Never forget
their approach, afternoon shadows
onward rolling of clouds,

earth's rotation unseen
through sunglasses,
imperceptible leaves falling from

redwoods standing the length of
the river. Never forget her
breath, finally stopped.

When they say "peace," this is what they mean—
face pale like slab of stone, lips slipping
apart, forehead warm to the touch.

To black this out—
how it happened and memory of it
two separate experiences blended into one—

would be to deny her existence. A daughter once,
a daughter now, even with her
absence. Shadows from branches

will always cast across the water,
whether she is there
or not.

Tip your gravedigger
By M. Ait Ali

The hours are gone

Whisked in rust-strapped cigarette ends—

Flicked away by fingers performing formal striptease gestures.

Now, it has been a long time

Since we properly lived an hour:—our fingers pinching on greasy touchscreens,

Zooming in on things quite knotty—zooming out of the thou-shall-not's

Of summertime betrayals—

Feeling magic in the nervous motion of words we couldn't articulate,

Menacing our phallic peace with photographs—not seeing much in them—

Yet deducing by worth of dust on noses that it's a valid truth

That the hours are, indeed, gone,—not even an hour was ours.

The dream is as cheap as a motel in the mega-bladder of nowhere,

Visited by the few:—Endured by none. West and east 'tween

The enslaving eyelids.

It's all we have: a dream to keep us sane or insane

Or both at the same time—a thought to chew on finding

More meaning in asking for directions to Slumberland.

We all carry on our faces

The look of the bewildered—Zebra day, father and lover
away—

All songs sung,—All hours done and forgotten but the tidbits
of surprise.

Our stains delicate and lively on blankets and pillows—who

Could have thought that they were going to be

Solely ours?

Selected Poems by Robin Gow

Thirst Trap

I am the water you've been looking for.
I'm asking for your burning.
Like night birds, my body is an image
for your passing. In a world of quick
likenesses I hope you pause here.
Thumbs, hoof-less in their trance.

Take a shovel to my back. Plumb
my chest for a diamond and my wrists
for a new kind of restraint. Teach me
where you've been all these echoes.
Tell me how long it's been since
you touched a photograph and I'll admit for me

it's been almost a year since I really laid
with someone. Found where the poses
lurked across our skin—crafted necessary idols.
If you make me gold, I'll do the same.
Statue of a boy in a bedroom's
dim light. Now, tell me what you want
to use me for? Be ruthless. Be eager.
I am ripe as a sick blossom.

Look Up

Despite their length
and girth,
this year no one is killed
by an icicle
(or so it seems).
I watched them lengthen

like angler fish teeth.
Drip in the sun.
Hold tight
in the frigid dark.
Opened my own mouth
and tried to get
in the habit of flossing.
Fishing ice from
between my teeth.
I have my own snow storms
now that it's almost spring.
Little cold parties
where I tuck my heart
in a mitten. I should
have kept better track
of the icicles diminishing—
instead, one day I looked up
and the rooves were clean
but slick from fresh melting.
Opened my mouth
to find all my teeth
still there. On my best days
I am much
less dangerous than
an icicle. No one
at all has died.
It is March.

Selected Poems by Bryana Joy

Nightingale

At any given time it's a tall order to find God
but in the spring of 1790, I know where I'd look first.
Back at Monticello, Sally is going on seventeen.
She strokes her taut belly in a room with no windows
and it's in that place I imagine the holy spirit is perched,
not dove this time but nightingale.

The nightingale is not what you expect.
Unlike the operas it inspires, it's no eyecatcher.
You won't notice it sitting brown in the coppice,
tucked up the way a homely secret is stowed in a great house.

Soon someone will be hollering "Push harder, child! Push!"
way down in Egypt land. Sally knows what it's like
to own nothing that can be touched,
not even her own fledgling body.

Not until you silence your large and well-lit home
will you hear it: up and down the swampy dark,
a thousand golden throats.

Baby Girls

at fifteen you pushed
a brittle-boned baby right out into a world
foggy with cigarettes and the empty words of boys

under the green and yellow walls

the green mold the yellow smoke

the TV droning always

baby girl don't let go
I want to say to her ittybitty fingers

but only you can say that

like your mama said to you
when she was fifteen too

in another tipsy tenement
shedding roofing like a drunk man drops his keys,
she said *oh baby girl*

how scared she was when she
bled you out into the world I think I know
I think I couldn't get a baby out of me without
gripping the hand of the man I love

oh baby girls
I want to take you home with me

all three

and put you in cradles around my bed

and wake in the night to feed you

I want the world to be different

there, I had a face & then I didn't
By Kaliyah Dorsey

after Danez Smith's "summer, somewhere"

we floats there, bears my lonely
a lone we. sometimes I hurts like a fake
ghost nobody had any ties to, but
you have to call it a family. insanity is
wearing the same face and expecting love.
disconnected kinship & a we without you,
knowing the fridge is empty then checking again in hunger.
in a dream where my I hums when the sun turns pink,
it carries what you & we didn't, couldn't, favors grape jolly
ranchers & wet berries.

Dogs
By Matt L. Hall

It's Saturday morning, and the neighbor's beagles are barking again. Their shrill sound in my ears makes me daydream of poison. I picture raw cubed beef tainted by injections of antifreeze. I imagine chocolate candies, naked of their crumpled silver foil, tossed by the handful over the eight-foot plastic fence where the mongrels can sniff them out and eat them and die.

When the neighbor, Sal, steps onto the porch, I poke my head out of the window. Under her eyes are bags the size of Buicks.

You gotta do something about those things," I say. I wave a finger toward the horrid creatures rooting in the grass.

"Go back inside, Phil. They're not bothering you," she says and tightens the purple strip of fabric hanging from her housecoat. She calls to the animals, but they do not respond.

"They're not even trained," I say. "What if they bite someone? I've seen them digging under the fence. They're going to get loose one of these days, and that's a lawsuit."

"At your age," Sal says, "you should know how to mind your own business."

I think of Kraft Singles wrapped around Contrac Blox, peanut butter cut with cornstarch and Borax—a squirt gun filled with Clorox bleach.

"It's inconsiderate," I say. "Very inconsiderate." Sal puckers her lips and makes kissing noises at the hounds.

"Come on, babies. Let's go inside." The beagles run toward her and continue into the house. As the dogs pass, Sal's housecoat opens just enough for me to notice the pale skin covering her collarbones. I think of Petra.

"Honestly, why do you need three dogs?" I say, but Sal shakes her head, then crosses her arms, and disappears inside. The sliding glass door rumbles. This noise is followed by the thick sucking sounds of metal meeting rubber and then the snap of the lock.

That afternoon I hear a raspy cough through the shared wall of our building. It isn't the first time. I think about rapping my fist on the wall, but then Petra's voice slithers into the back of my head.

"Be kind, Philip," she would say. Be kind. Those words always fell from her lips with unique elegance, as if wrapped in lace. Their delicate thrum somehow always made my anger seem childish.

What nobody tells you about marriage is that every wife has this power over her husband. It comes with the vows. At times, it was annoying, but more and more these days, I found myself missing it. That was one of our differences. When I was angry, I made sure the world felt it. Petra, on the other hand, didn't get mad very often, and when she did, that anger often evaporated without collateral damage.

"Maybe Sal should be kind and get rid of those damn dogs," I say, but Petra is not around to hear me.

She wouldn't have liked this place. This "community."

"We're too young to be stuck in some condominium surrounded by old people, Philip," she would say.

But with her gone, I couldn't stay in that cavernous house any longer. It was too cold, and every room had developed an echo. The floors moaned. The basement reeked of mildew. At least in this place, those sounds weren't the only option.

That night, I wake to a vivid red pulse on my bedroom walls. Sal's dogs are barking again, and I pull open the thick curtains with venom on my lips.

Outside, I see the dancing ruby lights of an ambulance and hear the shouts of two people, a man, and a woman, speaking in code. I watch them. Their navy-colored uniforms zip from the ambulance into Sal's home and back out again.

A spidery gurney emerges from the rear of the giant flashing vehicle. The wheels extend with a rickety pop.

The female medic pushes the gurney up the driveway, and the male follows. When they return, there is a figure splayed out on the stretcher—a shivering specter wrapped in a purple housecoat. It's Sal, holding a plastic oxygen mask over her face. I think of Petra.

The medics load Sal into the back of the ambulance, and then the navy-suited man climbs up beside her. The other medic slams the door.

This isn't the first time this type of thing has happened. Last month, it was the old couple in 6B, or one of them anyway. In this place, late-night ambulances seem to be part of the rubric.

Sal's dogs continue to bark.

When I can no longer sleep due to their raucous, I turn on the lights, dress, and make myself some coffee. Their noise continues. I pound on the wall.

"Shut up," I shout, but this only causes the curs to increase their volume. Their obnoxious baying continues for several hours until I am convinced they are barking out of spite.

The following morning I am still awake, drunk from the lack of sleep, and the noise hasn't let up. I expected someone would come to silence the creatures by now. Maybe one of Sal's relatives. A youthful son or a reasonable daughter who would take the dogs away. Someone understanding.

"Yes, I am so sorry those dogs have been barking all night," they might say. "Beagles are terrible, and I hate them as well. We'll take them to the shelter immediately and have them euthanized so you can get some sleep. We are so sorry for being inconsiderate. Here is some money for your trouble."

After two days, however, no one has come. Sal's ancient Toyota sits in the driveway untouched. Her mailbox bulges with circulars and clothing catalogs. There is a wet package on her front step.

I slide my slippers and jacket on and open my front door. A chill whispers across my face.

I march onto Sal's porch and pound the front door until the wall shakes. There is no answer, save for the dogs yipping and squelching from behind the courtesy window next to the door. The creatures jump and howl, their toenails clicking against the glass. I knock again, but still no answer.

I bang once more, but this aggravates the beasts into a frenzy. I tap an angry finger on the glass.

"You miserable creatures," I say and grip the brass doorknob in my hand. I expect stiffness, but to my surprise, the knob turns, and the door creaks open just enough to see inside. A trio of wet noses sniffs at the crack between the open door and the jamb. I hold a foot to the door so the beasts can't push through. I holler up the stairs.

"Sal, your dogs are barking again It's disturbing my sleep. I'm going to call the police if you don't do something about them.""

There is no answer. I shout again. Still no answer. I ease a shoulder into the home and am greeted by the pungent smell of sick, followed by the smell of feces.

I push past the dogs until I am standing in the foyer of Sal's home. At first, I am fearful that the dogs may try to bite me, but the creatures only bark a few more times then begin to whine.

"What"?" I ask, expecting some sort of reply. The dogs do not answer.

I climb the stairs to the living area. In the corner of the room, next to a window, is a hospital bed. Next to the bed sits a silver telescoping IV pole. On a wooden end table is a collection of orange medication bottles set up like chess pieces. I lift one to examine the label but do not recognize any of the names. I think of Petra.

I think of how those last few months gnawed at her cheekbones, how she was never warm enough. Petra would have had me put her bed in the same place—near the window—so she could feel the sun. I'd unfold a blanket across her frail shoulders and make her a cup of tea. The latter of which she would only take a few sips from before letting it go cold on the table beside her.

The dogs have defecated and urinated on the floor near the bed. In the kitchen, I find a roll of paper towels and press them into a huge ball. I drop it over the urine. I stack more paper towels and pick up the feces. Then, lifting the toilet seat, I drop the mess into the toilet and flush.

In the bathroom, near the bathtub, there are four empty bowls. When the toilet finishes its cycle, three heads crowd into the room. The dogs dip their muzzles into the bowl and slurp at the toilet water.

Three dogs and four bowls. The math doesn't make sense, but then I realize what the fourth bowl is for, and I lift it to the sink and fill it. One of the dogs sucks at the water and empties the bowl. I fill it again.

In the kitchen, I find a giant bag of dog food and a scoop and shovel kibble into the remaining bowls. The dogs chomp down their meal while I sit on the couch and watch them. Sal's phone rings. Without thinking, I pull the receiver to my ear.

"Hello?" I say.

"Hello, is this Mr. Ross?" asks a woman. The tone of her voice is as sharp as a bayonet.

I don't know a Mr. Ross. Was that Sal's last name? I had never seen anyone but Sal in her apartment. I didn't even know her last name.

"This is Graves—I'm Phil Graves—the neighbor. What is this about?"

"Mr. Graves, I'd like to speak to Mr. Ross, please."

"I don't know a Mr. Ross. I'm the neighbor. What is this all about?"

"Sal Ross, do you know a Sal Ross?" says the woman on the other end of the telephone. I can tell that she's getting frustrated.

"Yes. But I'm just the neighbor. I'm Sal's neighbor."

"Mrs. Ross has this number on file as her emergency contact. She's listed a Reginald Ross as her next of kin. It's very important that I speak with Mr. Ross."

"I'm just the neighbor. I'm taking care of the dogs. Of Sal's dogs."

"I'll call back," the woman sighs. The phone clicks.

I try to remember a time when I've seen someone besides Sal, but I can't. I've never seen another car besides hers in the driveway. It has always been just her—well, just her and those damn dogs.

I wander around the living room. On the end table next to the bed is a photograph. In it is a woman who looks like Sal, only younger. Her collarbones are displayed for the world while both arms adorn the waist of a tall, handsome man.

I assume this is the Mr. Ross the woman on the phone was trying to find. But why wasn't he with Sal? A ceramic urn on the mantle answers this question. At the bottom of the urn is a tarnished brass plaque with the name Reginald Ross engraved into it.

I let the dogs roam in the yard for a bit to use the bathroom and then call them back inside using the kissing sounds I've heard Sal make. Once they are indoors, I pat each one and fill their water bowl. I promise to return the next day. I make that promise again and keep it for the next three days.

When someone finally comes, it isn't a relative. It is a young black woman and a bearded man, both in police uniforms. They knock on my door, and when I answer, the woman asks if I know anyone who might have been close to Sal. I tell her that I'd never seen anyone coming or going.

I tell them about the urn and the barking and how I had only spoken to Sal when I complained about the dogs.

"Well, that's too bad," says the bearded officer after closing his notebook. "Looks like she didn't have anyone else." He shakes his head and stuffs the notebook into his pocket.

"Nobody?" I ask.

"Afraid so. She didn't have any children. We found a brother in Chicago, but he passed a few years back. You already know about her husband."

"What about the dogs? What happens to them?"

"We'll get Animal Control to come pick them up," he says. "You know the drill. Hopefully, someone will adopt them. One thing is for sure, you won't have to listen to them barking anymore."

"That's good," I say. A strange nervousness begins to creep into my chest.

"Yep. I know how annoying they can be," says the officer.

"What are the chances, though," I ask, "you think that someone'll—you know?"

"Take them? I mean, it's possible. People don't usually like beagles, though. They're loud. And that bark," the officer waves a finger in the air. "Well, you know what I mean."

"Yeah. It's—anyway, okay," I say. The officers thank me, and I watch as their car pulls onto the main road.

Once they are gone, I sit in my living room and try to read, but all I can think about is those creatures. How much I despise their shrill yawp. How that sound so often made my blood boil.

But somehow, the kettle under my skin doesn't whistle. I try to imagine creative ways to dispatch the mongrels, but nothing comes to mind. Instead, I think of Petra. When I don't hear the dogs bark for a few hours, I think for sure Animal Control has picked them up, and I panic. I rush over to Sal's door and find myself strangely relieved when three wet noses greet me.

I fill their bowls and sit with them for a while. I stroke each one and try to reassure them, but their eyes suggest only sadness and uncertainty. It's as if they understand that something has changed. The dogs lay at my feet, and I put my hands on my knees.

"God dammit."

I find three leashes hung in the basement, and one by one, I lead the dogs into my home. I allow them to roam freely. They sniff around for a bit and find a sunny spot on the couch. The three of them crumple together and fall asleep, their lips and feet twitching.

I retrieve their bowls and their food from Sal's house. I set the bowls up in my bathroom, just like they had been. I leave the toilet seat up—an affront that Petra would have playfully scolded me for. This time, I think she would have let me get away with it.

I sit with the beasts and listen to them breathe. There is unexpected comfort in their corn-chip smell. When the smallest one—Roxy is the name on her tag—squeaks, and growls in her sleep, I stroked her until she quiets.

"It's alright," I say to her, and she raises her eyes to look at me.

"Everything is going to be fine," I say.

Roxy sighs then puts her head in my lap. It isn't very long before she falls back to sleep.

Selected Poems by Carole Symer

Dear Invisible Stars & Cornstalks

You have your work cut-out:
                          my mind ice cold   like
          side-glancing Barbie.
                    Trapped
                          in my own dollhouse,
          sometimes
                    dreadful things come up.

A black cloud
                          a man's crumpled body   in red
                    & a lime green cornfield.

Imagine how his family felt
          a boy utters   unaware
          I am the man's family

                          although I haven't spoken to
          the carefree cousin on my mother's side
                              in the six months since
          the 6:03 a.m. train   stopped dead
                                        in its tracks.

Flashing lights, a crossbuck, a bell
                          & 172 long minutes.

Boy oh boy, go ahead & cry I tell us both
                                        Let tears float up
                    into the wet sky.

Cumulus: from Latin   denoting a heap
                                       of the simplest clouds
    included, occluded,
                              the ascent of unstable air.

Enter Scene

Start in the middle.

A train thunders
through a tunnel.

Screw backstory.

Fox scream or was it
the birds. Open one eye.

Make someone talk.

Damn, you were of such
consequence to me she said
kissing her.

Crank up the fog
machine. Conjure
lightning. Insert
a foreign word.

Step back, way back.
Try it again.

Force the scene.

Play the part that's
been cast for you.

Brash hissing
stage whispers.

Cut. End scene.

Gravida

From a backyard bruised by noon's heat,
        blood-root blooms,

here to where this day, this night
        this water breaks—

                pushed out into this world
        a mother's body, wilted like crepe.

Here, too, Gramma lifting you into
        the star-studded afterward.

Each inch in your climb through
        skin & eyes & lungs

        in reach of water & oxygen

                        & me, a floating cord.

Thoughts on moths and desire
By Nico Bryan

I'm sitting here,
thinking about the difference between moth and butterfly
realizing it comes down to being open or closed

i am the moth
wrapped in silk
feeding on thoughts of you at night

I cling to your luminosity,
flapping against brightness
tiny microscopic bits of powder falling around
the pattern of my wings just a diffraction of your light

sometimes their wings look like they have eyes or
just a brown dot swimming in the sclera,
orbiting a circular pool of umber,
across white canvas stretched out in the shape of an almond

my whole body splits at the seams
every time I try and retrace your eye inside my mind
and yet
despite the fray, I crave it

I once read that some adult moths never eat
and I think about what hunger does to the body,
the kind of hunger that's deep in the belly

warm and seeking
waiting to be satiated

Selected Poems by Kris Spencer

Of the styles of handwriting, and the direction of the lines written

> A natural unstudied hand, then, is the only true test of character – Henry Frith

(1) If it be even

Straightforward and firm, my
letters stand like soldiers of the
steel frame of the classroom's
cold window; keeping to the
lines I will walk in health and
be a rock and never look to be
this way or that; or be the one.

(2) If it be ascending

I am
the reaching
hand, scrambled
to for my ardour; lines
sloping up, ambitious to
spin away; wanting of form
and harmony, but firm and sure -
I will be called lucky, and be careless.

(3) The descending writing

Drooping downwards, with sad fingers

I will never pry or seek but stay home,
ungloved and grey-faced;
even if poked and bored,
and smothered I will
always yield and
give up to the
imagined
fear.

   (4) Unevenly made

Mine is formed by struggle: straight
to rise only to fall away,
unfirm and uneven; too fast to start
and then winded;
dragged down
by worry or bad luck;
summoned untimely
and hopeful early, prodigious –
I will be scorched and spotted
like a new leaf
in the frost.

Rotator Cuff

Is misguided gym snobbery denying you access to powerful

tools? - *Men's Health*

The movement of the big men
is delicate and precise; prescribed
by magazines and manuals,
and repetition. Like poets.
Nothing is lifted
or pulled absently.

They are careful, pernickety.
Exquisite.
Here, bodies are like cars
or aircraft.
Here, the big men train
in an ugly room
made noble by intent;
like a pirate ship
or a library.
I watch their etiquette
as they carousel
the free weights.
I choose the bench press machine,
shiny as a tractor.
The barbell is caged
between two steel tracks,
the movement prescribed
to an immutable vertical.
As I lower the weight
a lazy misalignment
plays metal against flesh:
gravity and simple force
(*mass* x *acceleration*)
tear my tendon over
and away from the bone,
elastic and tectonic.
The dropped bar slides
smoothly down the rails.
My pain is tenor, round and sharp.
No one notices.
In the changing room, I press
an ice pack to my ruined chest
as the big men, skittish and superstitious,
talk of how to get cut for competitions
with green tea and asparagus.

Selected Poems by Matthew S. Mayes

The Gentle Rose

Clean is the floor that the doctors scramble on,

momentarily free of tears stained red by

tonight's afterglow: amber vinyl,

many times they've met.

A precise violence not yet seen:

        remove soiled linen,

        dust,

        mop,

        sanitize,

        give a new face.

        In comes the next.

A young boy sleeps;

upon his bed he calmly dreams.

His face is pale, but shining;

hanging from its metallic arm

her rays fall on his skin like rain.

A gentle rose amidst the primal

he begins to stir, still tired from his inquisitive

leap toward the ground below.

The neighbor's son saw a superhero

jump from three floors up;

his mother claims the screen window must've been loose;

his father was mowing the lawn   *If only I had looked up*

44

I'm attempting to break our record:

    the one where we would

    toss the ball backwards

    toward that little crease

    in our arm and wait

    for it to jump back

Just like we would do when we were

    kids, in competition, seeing who

    could beat the "all-time record"

    that we decided was

    forty-four.

When our forever ends too soon, how does one

    traverse the unexpected present?

    A fox is in the henhouse, dressed

in glass, disguised as a friend.
The euphoria was
     your diaspora—a harmony
     of dreams.
This will be the last time we dance,
just like yesterday.

Selected Poems by Cindy Milwe

Dressing Room at 45

Unsurprised by the decline
of my flesh. Every useless thing

I did to keep this truth at bay--
all those miles across town lines,

finish lines, lines of cocaine
in the elevator at ballet class,

lines of boys and men from one side
of this country to the other, laps

around Central Park, Prospect Park
Griffith Park, Washington Square

and of course Lake Hollywood,
where you can't swim, but I did

my laps back and forth across
any public pool I could find

until my pinkies got pickled
by chlorine. And then I cycled

round and round, up mountains,
through canyons, always last

in the pack, shoulders hunched
at the wheel, a doomed racer.

Dance classes on Valium,
a marathon on Methadone

Tri-athletic masochism
in every ocean swim.

French Roast coursed
my anemic blood

as I barreled through Pacific
waves, peeled off my wetsuit

to a tan, ripped body
in a white string bikini

every morning at sunrise.
25 years later I pull huge

bathing suit bottoms over
the loose trunks of my thighs,

tug at the Lycra with an anger
I usually reserve for my husband

watching Sports Center
or porn. My son slumps

in his stroller munching
on cashews, grinning

at the miracle of my body,
the first house he knew.

But this End-Of-Summer Sale
strikes like a hail storm of grief,

Grandma Clara's Slavic arms
resurface from the dead

in every walled mirror.
"Wear it in good health,"

she always said at Bloomingdales
when she paid for a skirt or cardigan,

handed me the bag on the escalator.
Decades later, I decide on the same

black suit I've swum in for years,
hear Clara's phlegmy voice,

and watch my son stare
at the infinite story our bodies

can tell through a mirror.
"That looks good, Mommy,"

he says, eating a nut. I squat down
to kiss his hair, holding tight

to his words. I remember
my grandmother's wish:

"Wear it in good health."
And I wonder:

Is there anything
else I can ask for?

For Jay

You wander through my dreams
like a lost junkie—chest sunken

and strung out again.
Why the limp? The fat lip?

Do you enter to show me
how far I've come in love—

no longer the girl who adored you
and whom you forgot, who wore

dirty jeans just to smell you?
I see you on the faded couch—

stoned again in front the TV,
picking seeds from the heady

green clusters in the deep fold
of a double record album,

squinting, swigging ginger ale,
half-watching a rerun of Taxi.

I am no longer the girl you picked up,
slung over your huge shoulders,

and carried home on the "1" Train,
comatose from cheap champagne

and too many hash brownies
at that Christmas Party.

I am no longer the girl waiting

by the rotary phone, begging for you

to kiss the hollow base of my throat,
peel down my tights with your teeth.

The Man and the Boy
By Sabyasachi Nag

I don't think any of this would have happened if
Jasmin hadn't lost a girl, then a boy. She knew it was a boy.
That was some time back. Now we are in Rishikesh. Trying to
train the mind to deal with a lack, the entire month, like every
summer, for the last five years after she hit forty and doctors
asked her to stop trying.

Here at the Ashram, they teach you how to breathe,
love, grieve. We are exhausted. We don't see anyone before
checking out. Not even each other, until we are on the train
heading to Calcutta where my mother lives alone in the house
where I was born. Jasmin was born in Barrie. We are both
looking out the window.

They get on, the man and the boy, bent over, hauling
what looks like a heavy tin trunk; panting for breath, after
what seems like a mad sprint, up, then down a winding
overpass from nowhere to nowhere. The train has pulled in
moments earlier. The train would leave in a moment. They
seem to be sweating, or perhaps, it's the rain.

The boy is twelve or thirteen. From his smooth-as-
pebble face it's hard to tell. He's wearing a white Muslim cap,

as the older man, the kind I have seen Jasmin's father wear for prayers every Friday. The man's eyes, never resting on anything, moving up and down and sideways, inside deep sockets framed in dark circles, he seems to be searching something.

It's after eleven. The night spread out like a coat of black butter. We are passing the outer fringes of Lucknow – the cultural Mecca of medieval India. The train is running on time. The man and the boy find it hard to pull the trunk through the narrow corridors of the train car. Two bunk berths face each other across the width, and a bunk berth on the side, runs the length of the train like a spine, splits the coach in blocks, each block of six sleepers – a universe with a courtyard in between. Within the compartment there are no hard partitions, no hard divide, just curtains. The lights are coming on and off.

The man and the boy stop across the aisle in our compartment. They face the bunk berth on the side. It seems they have booked them both, but it's taken by two men facing away. The squatters seem to be fast asleep. They don't seem to have noticed the arrival of the man and the boy. There is someone everywhere, already. They try to move things under our berth so they can jam their trunk somewhere, forget about whatever is in it. There is no room. The trunk is too big.

The Conductor is already heading their way. He is wearing dark pants and white sneakers. He has a dark jacket on. Nothing fancy – the kind people wear with shiny nickel buttons and shoulder loops to give an impression of authority. Seeing him, the man gets busy, rummaging the deep pockets of his dark tunic for the tickets. The Conductor taps at the knee of the squatter on the lower berth. The squatter doesn't move, he is dead still. But the man and the boy wait. They have nowhere else to go. The Conductor's hand rocks the squatter's body, bringing it back to life.

The lower half of the Conductor's face, barring the space between nose and the upper lip, is covered in a rich growth of white beard that he has dyed in places, a kind of orange you get on your hands after slicing fresh turmeric. He has shoulder length hair, brushed from the flanks above his sideburns toward the centre of his head to hide a gaping bald patch. He looks over fifty. He is chewing betel. The squatter in the lower berth suddenly punts at the Conductor who is jabbing a clipboard into his feet. The board goes flying. The boy picks it up.

"This seat is reserved. Please find something else."
The Conductor's tone is polite, respectful. It seems he is used
to being treated this way; or that he knows something that
makes him respect the squatter.

"This seat is taken," the squatter says, "*you* find
something else." The squatter has a strong voice. It has woken
Jas. She looks at him. The squatter is facing away, toward the
window on his side of the night. The window with Jasmin's
shadow is dotted with splashes of rain. The rain flashes like
cinder as the train passes random light posts.

The Conductor is firm, the squatter won't let go.
People crane in to check in on the kerfuffle – the hoo-hah of
two grown men arguing over a seat. The man and the boy
watch the conductor, who's doing most of the talking. Jas,
wide awake now, watches the boy.

She stayed up the previous night practicing bottle tokes
between moments of extreme clarity. I was, too. I know how it
feels, taking in milk down a dark pit. I know she was making
something of it, the whole month, the darkness and the fact
that she is right on the edge. I look at her hands. She has the
hands of an artist – nerves spread out the back, like roots, dirt
lined up her gnawed nails – dirt from all the digging and
planting all week. *Trees like babies*. Jujube, mainly, that's

what we planted into the dirt; into our void. Because they live a hundred years and start fruiting at two. *One sure way to become grandma really quick.*

Her eyes are closed. Her body sways to the wobble of the train car. Her lips open and shut, purple from all the pot we smoked all month. Her shiny hair, parted on two sides like a rail-road cutting straight into the sky, blurred, as it trails down the horizon. I can't see that far, but I know. Right now, she has started to speak a strange cocktail of Punjabi, thick with Brampton North Park canuck. Her voice, just as strong as the squatter across the aisle. She can't help it. "Can you folks take it outside?"

What she means – let the boy sit, you assholes. They don't get that, of course. Or maybe they do, and they don't care. Or maybe they care, but they like her talking to them in that fashion.

The train has caught speed past a teeny lightless sub-station. I usually remember place names, but I am looking at the boy – our dead son would be his age. His brown eyes move gently between pauses, as if touching everything with a brush, touching it and leaving a mark. An hour and a half before the train reaches a terminus big enough to have lights on at the station where the Conductor can hope to have someone help him do his work. Perhaps there's help on the train waiting to be summoned.

The late monsoon has cooled the ground outside. You can tell from the smell. A chilly draught whistle in through cracks around the sealed glass. The wobble rocks the boy's hair. He has a face of a sand pebble. I said that. It seems the pebble has been rounded and chiseled and sculpted by a wild torrent for a long time.

"We can use another seat you know." The man seems quick on compromise. "Any seat. Anywhere else. We are all passengers, aren't we, every one of us?" He looks at Jas, for affirmation, I think. "It's only a matter of a night."

I know what Jas is thinking. She thinks he's a loser. I think he's playing nice, trying make a deal, get back to being invisible. Jas doesn't understand that. She is a straight shooter.

Just when it seems the man is ready to go away, just when everything seems to be settling back to the grind and hurtle of this train-universe, she opens her mouth, "Hello. You booked this seat, right? And this boy here has been standing, waiting?"

The man with the cap looks at her, annoyed, as if she spoke out of turn. And I think that's when everyone hears it too, a crack starting someplace you can't see, and then a ripple of cracks, as people move in their sleeper bunks just to get a closer look at Jas.

"Is this your seat," she asks the boy. The boy nods. "That man stole it. Steal it right back."

The boy says nothing.

"Take it."

No one says anything.

"Come on. Take it." The squatter in the lower bunk berth says, in a calm sotto, like a doctor breaking bad news. He straightens himself against the window, looks across the aisle, towards Jas. Her eyes are brown, almost like split cobnut with blue-black husk in the shape of eyelashes. Some kind of turn-on for him, I guess. He leans back on the window, flings his cracked feet the entire length of the corridor right up to the edge of my seat, crosses his arms and seems to say: "You don't even belong here you shitheads."

Then he turns toward the man, and the boy, and the Conductor, stopping to observe carefully, making a show of the care with which he observes. I can tell he's looking at the strange arrangement of the Conductor's hair, connecting the strange complexion of his beard to the Muslim cap on the man and the boy. I know. I have made that connection. I know what he is doing.

"You guys related? You guys brothers?" He says clapping the seat, making a shitshow trying to stop himself from falling over in fake glee – laughing at his finder's luck, as though it's a life-altering discovery.

"Let's go. We don't want trouble." The man is not looking at the squatter, but at the Conductor, this bearded train official, as if they were both tagged in some unspoken way, in a singular distress.

"Is there another place we can use? For the boy? I mean just the boy. He can't be standing up the whole night."

The man now looks at Jas, and keeps looking, as though, just by looking he could evoke a response.

"Don't do that." Jas says to the man.

As the man shuffles, the squatter grabs the boy by his arm, draws him close to his face. The boy is short. "Show me your ticket," he says.

"The ticket is with him." The boy points at the man.

"Come on. Pull it out." The squatter reaches for the man, staring into his eyes, not in the manner he was staring at Jas. It's different.

"That's my business, mister." The Conductor steps in, now with an acid voice. He's going to cut the squatter into pieces with his words.

"I don't like how you smell, man. Get away from me." The squatter says to the Conductor. "You have been eating something terrible. I can tell just from the colour of that thing on your face, man. You want me to be sick? In your face? Just get the hell out. And. Don't open that mouth again." The Conductor says nothing to the insult.

"Why don't you just let the boy have his seat?" Jas says.

"Veeru, you hear that?" The squatter in the lower berth slaps the seat again with his palm like he did a while back, like a child working a rattle.

"Your wife?" He asks me with a wink. I know what he's asking, but I suddenly feel the need to protect everything from him. I do a head bobble just to throw him off. I don't want to tell him anything. Maybe it's a mistake. It throws a fuse off Jasmin's head. I can tell.

"Talk to me," she says to the squatter.

The night's raging outside, lights are still coming on and off past abandoned outposts in the middle of nowhere. Other than the chemical buzz of the fluorescent, there is nothing else – not even the rattle of the train car – the sound of steel on steel has now settled deep inside the ear, like a worm.

"Your friend or wife?" The squatter asks me again. "You up or what?" The squatter says, not to me, but to the other man on the upper bunk berth. Not waiting for an answer, he taps the upper berth with his foot, hard, exactly where the other squatter is resting his head. He must know what he's doing because the kick wakes up the other squatter. That's when I realize what the Conductor has been trying to do. He isn't alone, this squatter.

"Why don't you go call the cops?" Jas asks the Conductor. "What are you waiting for?" She points her face toward the squatter as if to hold the threat close to his head. As if she found a gun and she is going to blow his brains out.

"Why don't you go call the cops," the squatter repeats after her in sotto, "what are you waiting for?". He looks at Jas and then back at the Conductor, accusingly, as if the Conductor has been delinquent at something he needed to have done long back – bring these tourists up to speed with how things work, here.

At first, I sense sarcasm, scorn perhaps. And then I look at the Conductor, his unruffled manner, prepared for every spin and turn, almost rehearsed, and the thought strikes from nowhere – what if all of this is rigged? What if the Conductor is the real faker? What if the boy's seat has been sold long before the train even started and what we are witnessing is just a show?

The Conductor gestures for Jasmin to stop. He doesn't want to leave anyone in doubt he is in control. Shaking his clipboard at the squatter he says something. I can't hear what he says. He's a fast talker. I don't understand. Or perhaps he begun saying something and then the train car wobbled and he bit his tongue.

The man up top has now moved. He is looking at Jas from his perch. I know his name is Veeru. When I was younger, that name use to ring a bell like Butch in Sundance. He stretches his legs under a white sheet that's pocked all over with brown stains. The stained sheet is crumpled against the blue of the rexine on the cushioned upper berth. He watches Jas from his perch and moves his hand under the sheet, rapidly, never losing eye-contact. She looks away. He laughs. Perhaps, at the absurdity of it.

"You drink brother?" Veeru asks the Conductor. "I got whisky." They laugh, both men on the bunk berth across the aisle, a guttural laugh.

"I will give it to you neat, bro. No water, no soda, no nothing. Just go back where you came from. Take your things. Hello. Take your things and take your brothers. I don't want you here. You understand? I will bring it to you in a cup. No shit. I promise. You said you want *no trouble*. Right? *No trouble?* Just go back."

There is a strange authority in his voice. It makes the man with the white cap look toward the exit, instantly, perhaps he remembers something, perhaps he remembers to forget something – about the other boy in the other train lynched just the other day – evening news packed with the blood-face of the sixteen-year-old – lynched, not too far from here – he was wearing his Muslim cap – this same white, like the boy, framed to the black of the head, and full of holes. Perhaps the man knows something. He turns around and walks toward the door, the Conductor follows. I look at the boy. I want to say to him – it happens. I mean, it has happened before, with other people, elsewhere. No big deal. But Jas has gotten a hold of him, the boy who started to follow the men. The boy is now torn. He seems to like Jas or he likes being held that way. He looks up her brown cobnut eyes. Perhaps he can see something no one else can.

"You stay here!" she straightens herself on the seat, making room. "Why are you following the men? You are not a man yet." The boy looks at her, stunned, as though he can sense something in her voice that he wants to keep, even though she isn't making sense to him.

"Here." She draws him close and hands her phone to me. "Call the emergency number," she asks me, foraging in her leather pouch, as if she means what she said, as if she really has a number on her. Then she grabs her black, thick rimmed eyeglasses, the shape of a trapezoid, clearly oversized for her lean face.

"You need a number to call bro?" Veeru looks at me from his perch, his eyebrows cocked, eyes shifting toward Jas. He seems to be in charge. I can tell, he knows something. He is now crouched against the ceiling of the train. He has uncrossed his arms. His cracked feet hang down the bunk berth. He is leaned forward, ready to pounce, I think, if I make one wrong move. He is strong. I notice the bulge of his ripped frame bursting out his slim-fitted brown half shirt.

Something about the way he says those words, the cold, ratchet pitch of a jackhammer breaking concrete, makes the Conductor stop and turn around.

"Do you really want the cops?" he says, drawing closer to this man on the top berth, looking him in the eye. There is something they both know, but the Conductor no longer cares.

"You hear him, Jai?" Veeru says, punctuating his words with a sound you make into a snot rag blowing dirt out the nose. The squatters have found a game. They want the Conductor gassed up like a tube man before they bring him down.

"Come here." Veeru says, staring down the Conductor from his perch, gesturing at his thigh, as if inviting him to an act they both know well. The Conductor says nothing to the insult. Meanwhile Jai has flanked his legs around the Conductor, jamming them to the steel ladder on the bunk berth across the aisle. Girdled between Jai's legs, the Conductor seems frozen; helpless, without voice. He stands still, looking at Jas, looking at the boy, looking a few feet away, at the man near the exit.

"Here, come on, do it." Veeru says, repeating the gesture around his thighs. The Conductor ignores him, tries forcing past Jai's flanked legs. Those are strong legs.

"You come this way, brother," the man says to the Conductor. He has come up the aisle to fetch him, but he is looking at the squatter on the lower seat, the man called Jai. He looks at him and shakes his legs wedged around the Conductor; shakes and stops, shakes again and stops, as though he is begging him to let go. Let go. Please. I beg you. We will be gone. Forever. Into the night. He doesn't say all those words. That's what I think is going on in his mind. Jai lets go, the Conductor and this man with the cap, they walk towards the exit, one trailing the other, without another word. But the boy doesn't move. He stays.

Jas is looking out the window. The wind is slapping in the rain pretty hard. You think you can hear the rain even though the sound of steel has taken in whatever it can.

"What's inside the box?" Jai asks the boy.

"You don't have to answer that." Jas turns to face the boy. "Where's your mother?" She asks, as if that instead was the right question.

"She's gone," the boy says.

"That man? He's your father?"

The boy nods, and then he looks at Jas, hesitates, as if he is unsure.

"Gone where?" She asks again.

The boy doesn't reply.

"And where are you headed?"

"To my new home."

"How long ago was she gone, your mother?" Jas asks.

"I don't know. I was sleeping."

"Gone, just like that."
"My grandma said, someone shot her."

"Really? Shot her? Who?" Jas says.

"Then the man came."

"You mean, that man, so he's not your father?"

"Grandma says I should call him father."

"You never saw him before? And your granny let you go?"

"She said there was nothing for me to stay back for. She said, I have to make my journey, claim what's mine."

"She didn't want to come with you?"

"She's old. She can't go anywhere. Besides, she said it was not her place, I have to do it alone."

"What are you going to claim?"

"Blood. My Grandma said my Great Grandfather used to be emperor."

"Of what?"

"You see that?" He points out the window. "All of that."

"All of it?"

"The entire thing. And then he went east. To Calcutta."

"And that's what your Granny says you should do? What was the emperor's name? The emperor has a name?"

"Emperor Wajid Ali Shah."

"Yeah? From history," I ask.

"Yes"

"The emperor who danced to his own score?" I look toward the boy then toward Jas, "I read stories about him when I was younger, he had three hundred wives."

"Open it." Jai interrupts, kicking at the tin trunk.

"Ignore him," Jas says, "and you have seen him? You have a photo?"

"I don't have the key." The boy looks at Jas.

Jai looks at the trunk, carefully. Then he pulls a claw hammer of out his luggage under the bunk berth and strikes at the lock, precisely. The lock splits open. The boy watches, as Jai pulls the trunk out to the middle of the corridor. It's dark. He throws a wild kick at the light panel, the lights come on, revealing on one side of the trunk, beautifully patterned layers of silk – sarees stacked tight. Using his hands, he scours in a frenzy, looking for something. He seems to know what he is looking for. Between the silk sarees there are other things – a robe, brocaded in gold; daggers inside leather sheaths, scabbed with what looks like fake gems; shawls – red, black; white pashmina; blouses made from velvet and taffeta; blouses with trim and frills; rugs with bright rose patterns; rugs with figures, scenes from war; silks threaded with gold and silver; and then a fake crown with a gold patina studded with one large stone that looks like some kind of amethyst. Then he finds a pair of black leather straps studded with small metallic bells.

"Whose are these?" Jai holds them up for Veeru to see. He is laughing.

"My mother's." The boy says.

"She was a nautch-nik?" Jai winks at me, co-opting me into something.

The boy nods.

"Yeah? You know how to put them on?"

"Yes." The boy says.

"You dance?" Jas asks. The boy nods.

"Yeah?" Jas blurts out loud, amazed.

"Everyone at home dances. Even my Grandma. We are the family of Wajid Ali Shah. It's in my blood."

Everyone laughs. At the boy. At what he just said. At the anklets that he has now taken hold of, that he is now holding out for everyone to see. Jas is looking at them in disbelief. I can tell from her eyes. I know what's going through her mind. She likes the boy. She wants to keep the boy. She laughs and holds on to the boy.

"Do you want to come with me?" she says.

"Where?"

"To my home."

"Where is that?" the boy asks.

"It's on the other side of the world," Jas says.

He shakes his head. "Yes," he says.

And she laughs. The hollow laugh of a penny in a tin can. I know that laugh. Strangely, everyone is laughing at the boy as he puts the black leather strap on his left foot, like someone who has done it countless times before. He does it without bothering to look – sliding the tiny prongs into the precise punch holes, easing the tips of the narrow belts into tiny loops – just by touching them. He is about to repeat the act on his right foot. His face washed in glory.

Just then, the man with the white cap shows up from nowhere. He sees the broken lock, he sees the trunk forced open, the boy holding up a dancing anklet, ready to put it on. He pauses. I see his body shaking, I don't know if it's rage or shame or fear, but he is shaking like someone took his clothes and he is cold. He looks at the boy's foot, shiny with the metal bells on the strap he had put on before. The man reaches for him, quietly. The boy transfers the other black strap he was holding between his tiny fingers, his face turned up toward the man, still smiling, hopeful, flushed with glory. The man takes the strap in his hand as though it was rightfully his. Then he strikes the boy's face with the strap, so hard, the boy falls over. In the stunned second, the man looks around, meeting everyone in the eye. The boy gets up and looks away – his moon smeared-pebble face – darkened with the marks from the blow.

Before anyone realizes what happened, Veeru jumps down from the upper berth into the aisle, letting the full weight of his body bear on the shoulder of the man with the cap, instantly bringing him down to the floor.

And Jai, as if waiting for a cue, leaps out of his seat, lunges ahead of the torso of the man sprawled on the floor. Then he starts dragging the man's body by the collar. Dragging it toward the exit of the train. Veeru, lifting the man from the rear, by the waist, and Jai dragging. Then, they take turns kicking feverishly at the man's hands trying to grab anything - the steel trunk, the steel ladders, the steel of the bunk partitions further down the aisle. No one says a word.

By now Jas has taken the boy in her arms, crudely, as though she had found what she has been missing all this time, as though it were for her to give the boy what he doesn't know belongs to him. And she doesn't know either, how or what to say that. The boy is still. He is looking out the window. He is looking at the night outside, as if it was his own. As if he has been out there before.

Jai and Veeru are still working on the man. They have dragged him close to the exit. It seems they are going to throw him out of the train, without another word, in a manner so smooth, it seems they have practiced it. It seems they have been waiting. It seems everyone has been waiting - whatever it was – everyone wanting for it to get over fast so they can put it in the past and go back to sleep.

Just then the Conductor hurries in. He holds on to the man's feet; he tries to stop the squatters. The Conductor is strong. He wiggles his body into the steel of the bunks and tries to hold the squatters off with everything he has. But the two men are unstoppable. Today they have a different kind of power.

I look away. I look back at Jas. For a moment I think I see her clenched jaw. For a moment it feels she wants too for those squatters to do to the man what he did to the boy. The marks on the boy's face have settled.

On the far end of the train car, Jai is wrestling the door, trying to balance the weight of his body as he stands on the man's face, his cracked feet digging and twisting, as he works the jammed bolts. And when the door flings open, a ton of wet air rushes in and Jai, as if he were expecting something else, is thrown off; in the power of the wind, he meets his match.

The Conductor stands watching Jai, as he hurtles forward, face first, out the train's opened exit, like a strawman, halfway down the footboard, head popping out. Just a tap, and he would be on the roadbed – the rain-washed smooth of the down tracks, shining, vibrating, sliming in and out of itself.

Even in his fall Jai has managed to have his legs wedged on to the man's head, his crotch jammed against the man's neck; arms flailing for grip against the steel handle outside. He is so close to the girders I am sure he is having to flinch to keep the cinders from the train wheels getting into his eyes.

The mad wind is pulling them both down toward the cinders. The man's head, wedged between Jai's legs, they are both slowly sliding. I stand behind the Conductor, helpless; staring. Maybe that's how justice happens. I don't say it. But Jai's friend, this other man called Veeru, he has now joined forces with the Conductor, trying to stop the man with the cap from sliding down any further – the same man he was about to throw out the train. By doing that, he thinks, he can hold on to Jai from being blown to the wind. He holds on to the man's waist, he winds up in knots against the walls of the train car, against the steel of ladders; against angles and poles; resisting the drag of gravity, resisting the wind, resisting the spell of the down track slipping past in great hurry.

Together with the Conductor they pin the man to the floor, before pulling him back inside, the man with the cap, and with him, Jai, wrapped around his crotch like a chain lock. Then the two squatters, without another word, head back to their places. The man with the cap lies faceup on the floor. His jacket ripped, shoes off, shirt soaked in grime, blood oozing out his nose.

"The man's bleeding," someone says.

"I have first aid in my carry bag," the Conductor says.

"You stay here with me." Jas says, refusing to let go of the boy's hand, snuggly wrapped around hers. I notice the open trunk with the emperor's things getting in everyone's way. I pull it back inside.

Selected Poems by Olivia Piper

Calf Poem (I Wonder)

Are there calf skeletons in the pond,
the one by the lonely tree about to pitch itself into the water -
I wonder, as I drive by the pasture.

There are three or four live cows, massive brown beasts
and one calf standing alone by the tree.
It gazes into the water at the squiggly calf staring back,
I wonder if it thinks it's a friend, if it wonders why it doesn't
come home.

The pond looks deep and I think there must have been a calf or
two
who wandered too close to the edge and was lost.
I wonder if the cows remember the sunk babies,
if they refuse to eat the dandelions and bloodroot growing by
the edge of the water
like flowers on a gravestone.

I pull over to look it up: cows have a memory span of six
weeks -

Thank God
I say out loud.

By spring they will no longer be living in a graveyard,
they will have forgotten it all, just in time for new calves.

You'll Never Get Away from the Sound of the Woman that
Loves You

After "Silver Springs" by Fleetwood Mac

I am standing in the back room of your mind
turning a lamp on and off until the bulb burns out.

I will not be forgotten,
even if all I am is the after image when you close your eyes -
burned into your memory.

A laugh that carries you home,
a song you can't unhear,

a shock of light.

Sonnet (on a photograph)
By Justin Lacour

There's a photograph you
posted of you w/a dog & a snippet
of backyard. You've got tortoise rims,
your hair tucked up in a newsie's cap.
Your face. Brighter than the yawp of songs.
So I sit here w/my gray hair & flannel,
my desk job & my little cigars, playing a
guitar of rubber bands you can't hear.
You once said "The graffiti I want keeps
dancing & rearranging & writing itself
into something we can't understand." Just so,
your picture walks me right up to the edge of what
makes sense. A place where the wind blows through
my clothes & the forest closes silently behind me.

Snakeskin
By Alex Mika

The snake is gone.
It has left behind a sleeve of scales
In search of a tabula rasa.
What good is a clean slate to a snake?
What did it sacrifice besides its skin that day?
How many sins rest in skin?
How much knowledge? An apple's worth?

Memories lie locked in those circular
Honey cells; a thousand eyelids that will never
Open again.
They have been written on this papyrus
With venom, for it lasts much longer than ink
And cannot be deciphered by any known Rosetta Stone.

One autumn, this scripture will decay
Or burn like Alexandria's library.
In swirling wisps of smoke,
A shadow of a tongue will flick
The glowing embers into the sooty sky
And gift the heavens with new celestial eyes.

Selected Poems by Michael Waterson

Astrology Digest

Scanning my horoscope over breakfast,
I find it inauspicious:
Don't look to resolve big questions today.
The answers will have to wait.
I sooth dispiriting soothsaying
with a bite of toast and science,
recalling Ptolemy's Zodiac wheel
got skewed a month down the centuries
by our planet's wobbly tilt.
Astronomy says the firmament's unfixed;
the outlines of astrological signs
will be unrecognizable eons hence.

Turning a page, I read
about a study that posits the brain,
with its galaxies of neuro-nets,
replicates the universe in microcosm,
a model antipodal to our modern bent,
but one into which the Hellenes, who
reckoned all from the human angle,
would have leaned.

Like the stars that we look up to,
will those neuro constellations realign,
dream up new overarching beacons
of our destiny, or will old ones still outshine?
Will a new gray matter Zodiac
dissolve our nebulous terrors,
our black holes of despair,
usher in an age light-years beyond Aquarius,
satiate the heart's hunger
for kinship with the heavens?

My stomach, ruled by my sign,
pulls me down to Earth,
where there's a matter more consuming:
keeping the cosmos twinkling in my skull.
Following the oracle's advice,
I dig into my victuals, leave larger questions
where I found them, dangling
between synapses in the stars.

Monumental

My son, with other tourist kids,
perches atop the capstone
of a dolmen, a Stone Age portal tomb,
surveying the barren austerity
of West Ireland's Burren, as I wonder
how flesh-and-blood manhandled
tons of limestone.

My guidebook notes
ancients supposed giants
erected these megalithic memorials.
Since science exiled giants to fairytales,
parsing monumental mystery
invites scientific fancy:
interstellar visitors of high intelligence
intervening in our little lives,
leaving weighty evidence
of their presence for our edification.

Is it more down-to-earth averring
bone-deep hunger for light
hoisted these humongous homages,
slabs sanctified by blood, toil, tears?
Can this unyielding place yield proof, when—

aided by a pint or two, or no—
whimsey still spies wee green men
born of lightning jigs,
will-o-the-wisps leading us on,
despite our modern grounding?

The guidebook tells us origins
of these massive puzzles
of will and muscle
remain unknown,
as our children laugh
and clown for photos,
bright mementos, like constellations,
distant pinpoints of light
shining from the infinite
darkness of which we
remain so unenlightened.

Down Home Bluegrass
By BJ Fischer

My grandfather hosted two parties every year at his house in the country and we were there every time, starting when we were babies.

Grandpa was a lawyer—not a rich one, he worked for the public defender's office. His clients were people who did it, he used to say. He was raised in a West Virginia coal mining town, a place somewhere between *The Waltons* and *October Sky* (again, his words).

One of his parties was around Christmas and the other was on the 4th of July, where we grilled hot dogs, churned ice cream, and played softball with our bi-annual cousins. After dark, we would gather around a campfire and grandpa would bring out his banjo and he'd play and we'd sing along.

I remember the warmth of the fire on my face as he sang this into the purple night air:

> *I was on a dusty road*
> *Far from my blessed home*
> *Looked up in the dark black sky*
> *The moon looked down on me*

I know my Momma's sitting home
Rocking on the porch
And maybe she's wondering
What did become of me.

I can't hear the dinner bell
I can't hear her sweet voice
But the moon I see above me
Is the same moon she can see

I was driving cross-country for Grandpa's funeral when I heard this song on the radio.

It's first chord indicted me for my venal life. I was a sinner who had lost his last chance to repent.

See, when we were little we loved the sing-alongs. We waited all day for them; we begged grandpa to get the banjo. We sang the choruses in full throat.

As we got older, though, we found the whole thing lame and ridiculous.

And ridicule we did.

There was another song with animals in it and they were referred to formally, like "Mr. Flea" and "Mrs. Possum" and when we got to be teenagers we'd walk around all day inventing new things to call each other, like "Mr. Maggot" and "Mrs. Slug." When grandpa was out of earshot, we'd mock him, using a branch for a banjo and howling like a dyspeptic hound. We'd make up lyrics and laugh until we cried.

When he did sing, we could not have rolled our eyes harder than we did. Once we had cars we begged our parents to let us leave.

It wasn't just that. I moved to California to create video games in our historic games division. Mostly, I did World War II games. My job was in environmental design—the towns, the villages, the bridges, and the shops where the battles happened.

A vet told me once that the only thing missing was the total terror. We laughed about that. Who buys a game to feel terror?

At parties, after it had gotten late, I entertained the masses with an imitation of my grandfather at the campfire. I'd use a ladle or a squash racket for the banjo and I'd sit on the floor and howl and yodel. I had a repertoire of mock song lyrics, each of them belittling. You date your cousin in my songs.

People loved it. They *begged* for it.

The nice thing about a cross-country drive is that almost anything can be considered "on the way." Including Tug Fork, West Virginia, where grandpa had grown up.

I had never been to West Virginia but I was going in with my eyes wide open. I had seen the photo essays and read the elegies. I rode into town thinking that Grandpa's songs were noble ballads from a dead culture and I was an archaeologist visiting the ruins.

It wasn't like that, though. It was kind of like that, but it wasn't.

I parked my car on the street. There were weeds in the sidewalk cracks and the house I was parked in front of appeared to be in danger of imminent collapse. But the house next to it had a white picket fence and wind chimes, a perfectly mowed lawn, and flowers in bloom. A woman was on the front step sweeping and I waved to her and she smiled to me and waved back. She wasn't even smoking a pipe.

Down the street a little I came upon a tavern and entered, pulling the screen door and hearing it creak as it opened and slam behind me as it closed. The bar was empty except for the clean-shaven and young bartender who was talking on the phone and limping back and forth behind the bar.

I sat at the bar and he put a napkin down and when he finished his call he came over to me, rolling his eyes.

"Never ends," he said, "what can I get you?"

"Rye," I said.

He pushed the glass across the bar. "I'm Scott Antonelli," he said.

"Martin Taylor," I said.

"What brings you to town, Martin."

"It's a long story."

"No one gets here at the end of a short story."

"Ok, then," I said, draining the rye and pushing it back to him. "Like I said, my name's Martin Taylor. My grandpa was from here. He had moved north to be a lawyer. Public Defender. Anyway, he died last week. I live in L.A. and I was driving over for the funeral and thought I'd take a minute to see what Tug Fork was like."

"Sure," he said, filling up my glass. "The Taylors lived over on the other side of town, down the hill a bit."

"Did you know 'em?"

"Yeah, I'd say I did. They're all gone now. Last one left was Eleanor who died maybe nine years ago, just before I left for Afghanistan. Probably be a cousin."

"Had to be, his siblings all passed first," I said.

We shared an awkward pause.

"So you're a local," I said.

He smiled. "Born and bred. We were all miners, going back as far as you could. Fought for the Union, that far back. I was a pretty good student and I joined up right away to go the sandbox. Left the lower part of my right leg on the left side of a dusty road. Came back and got my business degree from WVU in Beckley and then came home. Own this bar, the grocery stores in the three towns around here, and a transportation service."

"You're not what I was expecting," I said.

"You expecting a guy with a leather vest and a long, grey beard? I could find a guy like that."

"No need," I said. "What were the Taylors like?"

"I was afraid you'd ask me that. You know, I have them just blending in. Going to Church. Playing football, on the line, not all-conference or anything like that. The place where they lived is even gone—it was a green house with a big garage where they had a woodshop, but they put the new branch campus of the community college there."

"Music?"

"Nothing I recall. Lots of people here play a little. Why, someone make it big?"

I sat back and looked up at the ceiling. "No," I said, choking. "Grandpa used to play bluegrass for us at family occasions. That's all."

He reached out to grab my hand. "Well, that's a memory to hold onto," he said.

"Yes, it is," I replied. "That's the problem."

He took his hand back and let that last part carry off in the distance.

"Was he singing about here?" I asked.

"No man, everyone thinks that." He moved over to a bulletin board to the far side of the bar and he brought back a poster for a bluegrass show being held that night, down at the town square.

"If you can hang out 'till then, you might find what you're looking for."

So I did. I took a long nap in the car and when it was time I headed over to the town square.

The gazebo sat in the middle of the square and it set the scene, that's for sure. It was the gazebo of another time and a larger town…the inside of a Victorian snow globe, with a cupola and shingled dormers and eight small arches along the roofline, each of which curved over a painted vignette of West Virginia history. Latticework connected each of the structural posts and gave a delicate feeling of lace; the baluster was white picket and was, like the entire structure, freshly painted and gleaming in the twilight.

About fifty people were sitting on the lawn on their garden chairs, waiting for the start of the show. I had expected a monolithic wall of hillbilly, but the faces I saw contained long beards and crew cuts; were mostly old with some younger, even some black folks, almost as if the whole group had been placed there by an ad agency.

I didn't have a chair and was about to sit on the grass when Antonelli waved to me; he'd brought one for me—it was nylon with a beer logo on it—and we sat. I saw an old man—very old—wandering around the side of the gazebo and I waited for him to pick up his banjo and head to the stage but he didn't and the next thing I knew there was a man on the stage who wasn't an old man but a young man.

Truth be told, he was my age, which made the whole thing even more personal. He was wearing horn-rimmed glasses, an ill-fitting plaid sportcoat, a bright white shirt, and a narrow black tie; a kind of Grand Ol' Nerdy look. Was it so off-point as to be affectatious or was it an honest statement?

He began to play. I wish I could say I transcended directly back to Grandpa's backyard, wading in the river of time to wash away my sins, but that wasn't what happened. For the first few songs I sat among the audience, and they were swaying gently and clapping their hands and I was embarrassed to be among them, a weed in their garden of song. I couldn't bridge the estrangement and I sure fate was going to withhold from me a second chance at what I had forsaken.

The next words I heard were these:

My home's on the Shenendoah

My home's on the Shenendoah
My home's on the Shenendoah
And I never expect to see it again

I opened my eyes and looked around and saw what my grandpa saw when he sang that song, the mountains, and the trees in silhouette, the faces front and center. Wars stopped and birds stood quietly in the trees.

The singer finished the song and he was talking to the crowd and I was floating on clouds and not paying much attention to what he was saying. I was aware a moment later that everyone was looking at me and Antonelli was patting me on the back and I looked up and saw a plaid arm pointing and waving and gesturing for me to come up to the stage.

I looked at Antonelli and he was nodding at me, so I stood up, somewhat unsteadily, and walked down the center aisle and up the stairs.

I stood next to the singer. I noticed his teeth, which were surprisingly straight.

"Who do I have here?"

"My name is Martin Taylor,"

"And where are you from?"

"I live in L.A., but I grew up in Spring Brook, near Buffalo."

When I said L.A. there was a soft gasp in the audience and he responded right away. "L.A.!" he shouted, "let's give the man a hand. And what brought you to Tug Fork from L.A.? Makin' a movie?"

"No sir. My grandpa was from here, and he passed a couple days ago and I was driving over to his funeral and I thought I'd see where he grew up."

"I'm so sorry to hear that. What was grandpa's name?"

I told him and he looked out at the crowd. "Oh sure," he said, "I remember the Taylors. Good people. Bet someone here knew Roy Taylor. Anybody?"

Two or three hands went up and everyone clapped, including me. A woman in the middle of the crowd shouted out. "I went to school with him. Everyone called him Lefty."

Which I had never heard.

"Martin, I understand there's a very specific memory of your Grandpa that you carry with you."

"Yes, sir," I said. "We'd have campfires at his house, and he'd get his old banjo out and sing bluegrass songs. I think it reminded him of his life here and this town and all the people—old times, good times. I can see why."

"How about that, keepin' the beautiful stuff alive, all the way to Buffalo. God Bless his soul," the man said. He zeroed in a little bit, move a little bit closer. "What kind of memory is that for you?"

I took a deep sigh—deeper than I expected I would—and then I took another. My instinct was to keep all my venality hidden, but I looked into the eyes of the people attending a bluegrass concert in Tug Fork, West Virginia in 2019 and it just seemed like this was a place where the flawed and broken down was safe and for once I should just say fuck it and stop running from the truth.

"It's bittersweet. See, as we got older, we made fun of Grandpa for signing those songs. I feel so bad about it right now and I wish I could go to him and apologize."

A tear slid down my cheek.

Jim put his arm around me. "Martin, let me tell you something," he said. "Bluegrass is about the goddamn most bittersweet thing there is. Bluegrass is like Church, it's there because people ain't perfect. Grandpa woulda known that."

He paused for just a second.

"Tell me a song he sang."

"The Moon Looks Down," I said, barely able to say it.

The crowd clapped. "Arright Martin, I'm gonna sing that one, but we gotta make a deal. I need you to sing along. Deal?"

I nodded.

When he played the first chord, I shuddered. I choked a sob down...

I was on a dusty road
Far from my blessed home
Looked up in the dark black sky
The moon looked down on me

I barely garbled out the words, but the audience was with me, singing along and I felt a lift and I and I discovered my voice—a green shoot from a charred stump--and it rang out and the people in the crowd clapped. I was soaring through the mountains watching the sullied earth below me as the feathers on the tips of my wing rippled in the wind.

I can't hear the dinner bell
I can't hear her sweet voice

But the moon I see above me
Is the same moon she can see

He finished and the people clapped and he leaned over and gave me a big hug. "Bless you and the Taylors," he said.

I was crying again.

He whispered into my ear.

"Son, Roy was the last of the Taylors, right?"

I nodded.

"Then there's no one else to tell you and I want to make sure you understand, son. Understand what you were hearing from Grandpa. It wasn't nostalgia. It was a curse to work in a brutal job and have your kids be desperate to get away and then to wonder about the ones who don't, so you feel bad about that, too. Everyone suffers. The vulnerable—the ordinary—suffer more, they always do. That's what he was singing about. People of comfort never wrote any bluegrass music."

We locked eyes for a moment and he patted my back and I walked off the stage and off into the park. I heard the music behind me and I didn't stop and I got to my car and I drove straight to Spring Brook, the moon asking me who I was.

I got to the funeral home about an hour before the visitation. I walked in the front door and they were getting ready, primping and fluffing. No one from the family was there yet. I saw the casket where he lay. They had leaned his banjo against the foot end. I walked across the room and crouched down and looked at it.

The head was black from use and I reached out and ran my finger over it.

Wishing Bone
By Paris Jessie

tossed to the ocean, go
face-to-face

down close
as a landing strip

in one breath, rest
give your best side

cool as untouched pillow
breathe, again

prepare to whisper
close enough for a secret

all the memories
of the "once was"

the tide eats them up
whole

pulled away
to go where they may

they are in the hands of
mother nature, now

cleansed with ocean
cold with moon

hot with sun
hung with stars

rock away
out of space, or

outer space
unseen, but thought of

the horizon blurs
mixes it all

surely you see how
water glistens and trembles

but the body still leaks of
bruises and aches
for now

Selected Poems by Christopher Louvet

The World Is Perfect This Way

Sleep goes easily
as it comes.
Foxtail palms, panic-

grass, and sea oats
scaffold somniloquies
on snoring winds

that loosen teeth.
The sea unsleeping
too casts up

the strand a sleeve
for shattered bones,
a way to explain

the world is perfect
this way. Sharks
enlivened by hunger

revel their wild
in wonder both
bioluminescent

and ancient. Sleep
comes easily
as it goes.

Wait, night will
concede. Wait,
the tides will

begin to cleave.
Wait. The sun will
intervene but

refuse to explain.
The world is
perfect this way.

Last Winter

Nobody adjusted
the building's
timed exterior
lighting to match
how early day-
light leaves us.
Next door, fenced
and mostly razed,
one of the first
structures raised
on this beach in
the early 1930s--
the Surf Club, soon
a Four Seasons--
remains in shoulders,
ribs, and spine
only, gutted to
the villa's Dade pine
timber and 80-year-
old brick arches
shored against
bedrock drilling.
The earth shakes
to exhume more dust.
A chill arrives
in late December.

Desiccated palm
fronds claw at
our front door
most mornings.
The sea ripples
with jelly clouds
and yellow and
brown seaweed blooms.
Every night the
exposed ruins flood
with halogen
light while tower
cranes stand sentry
and, like us,
excavators thirst
in their sleep.
By day, Bobcats
prune naked the dune.
One week of cold's
all we'll remember.
We'll move out.
Our building will
be sold by summer.

Pareidolia

Always the hottest summer on record,
the year's established rhythms crumple,
tangled in blackberry brambles
forgetful enough to bloom in June.
Peonies in their drift disintegrate
in the season's first storms.
They're left distraught,
disheveled as a mind
seeking asylum from asylum,
unthinking, unmovable.

With so many restrictions
in place, the construction's
completion will be delayed.
When the school year resumes
we'll have no place to stay.
The past is not a truck
that swerves on the highway.
Traveling in the same direction,
we don't see it coming.
Too preoccupied extracting faces
from clouds and house facades,
smoothing from the mirror
hidden messages only we can read,
trying to remember the name of the song
not on the radio or stream but
that melody we hear everywhere we go,
we don't see it as it overwhelms
until ensnared by its undertow.
The mind seeks asylum from the mind.
Mimetoliths, all named Bartleby,
astound in concert with
their agony and deep reserve.
We should be so stoic.
The world after all is human,
too human, an absolute chaotic
disaster with a long arc,
and it's our fault, all of it,
but especially its humanity,
our burden and best hope.
The evidence accumulates and abounds.
Even our computers shuffle
their decks of understanding,
alive to the Rorschach world
as they know it, all data unwound
from a single point
in the ambient overflow of conspicuous patterns

even as yet more patterns go unrecognized.
The observed depends upon the observer,
but why does nobody ever talk about how
now the observer depends upon the observed?
Rough as a tongue, the sense of time, startling
as a baby cockroach with a smile on its back.
The carnivals of our modern life
with their arresting sideshows
clown about our screens
like faint straight lines
on the surface of Mars,
canals of sentience, long
breaths of impermanence.
The dream of what could
have come after what might
have been, what maybe did
after what maybe was, but
not here, not now, shatters
in static and snow,
many worlds collapsed
to the hand gripping a doorknob,
to the finger pressing a button
in an elevator, no future trail
that is not now, no fork, no exit.
Even my shadows go mad,
unsure if I'm weasel or whale.

Selected Poems by Julie Benesh

The Household Hierarchy: Whereby all Beings Act in Accordance with their Nature, Unintended Consequences Ensue, and Mercy Remains Essential

Mom let me rescue Sam the guinea pig from 5th grade bio.
We put his cage on the top shelf of the built- in bookcase in the living room,
Right up near the ceiling.

After a few weeks of detente,
Tabby Cleo hurled herself from the back of the rocking chair to the
Bars of his cage, a furry loop
Clinging by her 20 claws.

She couldn't get to him; Nor could he, shrieking like a bird,
Escape.

We detached her, and whisked Sam's cage
To the privacy of the utility room,
Where the next morning found him
Lifeless.
Either the furnace gassed him, or the shock precipitated
A delayed heart attack.
No autopsy performed; no charges filed, nor civil action taken.

Corpse Pose

At the end of the day, on my way to yoga, the sun is yet to set, and no crepuscular rats dart through snowbanks like they did the night before, so far as I can see; the days are getting longer.
First to the studio, I take my favorite spot, at the end, where I

never used to want to be; hot yoga which I never used to think I'd like, but I love the routine of it unspooling as always: child's pose, sun salutations, lunges, warrior sequence, forward fold, tree, pyramid, goddess, locust, crunches, bridge, pigeon, happy baby, twists, legs up the wall. I sip my water and lie down for *savasana* imagining the sweet, spicy chai I will brew when I get home, and an essay I wrote this morning and I wonder whether a word I used was I word I shouldn't have used, in that essay, and I am only supposed to think about "now," and my breathe and my easeful body, not Past Essay and Future Chai, then it occurs to me, a word is just a word, and "now" can be longer, much longer, than the time it takes to walk two blocks through the snowy streets and brew a cup of chai, long as a late winter's evening, long as a life.

Head to Toe

I'm not a girl, I'm a management consultant and professor of middle-aged students who call me doc when I wish they didn't. Yet I remain known for my hair and footwear, then and now.

Then, as expected: shiny surfaced middle-parted chestnut brunette. Saddle shoes red v. black. Clogs. Goth boots. Edged out peers. Later: blonder, smarter, more degreed. Wiser, grayer; hence, with assistance, blonder. Smarter meant better jobs; more money: better shoes and hair—virtuous cycle.

Now: what's beneath the scalp and skull, expected, (more or); less so platform snakeskin wedge-heeled booties on fleet feet of forever nerd with fierce blonde mane that at height of heels, peak of highlights, a tipsy C-suiter-suitor said he wanted to wear, like a pelt, on his belt.

Spun, shocked, sobered—thought he'd appreciated *inner* brilliance.

Knew then, I'd be sad when hair, footwear, would inevitably descend to finally full-on sensible, but goddess must, at every cost, preserve the feet for firm and mobile foundation, the mind above all else.

trouble the river *(for bay bay)*
By Durell Thompson

Yes, he died
Young. But Death doesn't
Really have an age bias.

The Baptist say hell is hot.
The Orthodox say hades is dark.
I say it's all the same.
And Jesus is a brown
African with braids.

I pray that we live
Long enough to
Say, *we*
Didn't give
A damn,

I pray that
We live long enough to
Say, *that we shitted*
 On Them.

Yeah, *we shitted on them,*
Crossed Their
Redlines
With black faces
    Jamming Nipsey
    Ghost riding our four
    Door sedans
With a diamond…

In the back…

A diamond to our backs...

Tipsy on

Salt. Water. And somebody's. Hallelujah.

To End with a Flourish
By DB Gardner

The moment the whine of the big tires over pavement gave way to the low growl of stone, the bus driver saw the girl's pale blue eyes ice over. Even the natural wave in her auburn hair seemed to straighten. Sumac branches slapped the side of the thirty-foot whale, and Myra eased the yellow beast into the center of the narrowing road, the engine shifting lower as they crested the hill. In the overhead mirror, she again found the girl: her bloodless cheek pressed against the window, wearing that same vacant look most children wore on their way *to* school. Yet each morning, this one bounded onboard as if sprung from a trap, a tuft of blue aster, or Queen Anne's lace over one ear.

Dust rose from either side of the lumbering machine, stones popped away from the wheels. At the bottom of the hill and around the next curve, Myra knew the girl's mother would be waiting to wave her down, cigarette dangling listlessly at the tip of her lip, animal-hair wet and tangled, a fleshy arm draped over the mailbox. Acid swam in her stomach as she spotted the rose-print housecoat through the swale; the woman had stepped into the road to stamp out her cigarette. The bus halted with an airy squelch, engulfed in a sand-filled fog at the mouth of the drive. She threw open the door, but the plastic flip-flops had already started up the overgrown path, a sweat-stained hem swishing in time with her thundering steps. Myra's eyes went to the mirror. "See you Monday morning," she said softly to the girl.

The child gathered her belongings in a daze, scrambled from the bench, caught her foot on the seat leg, and went sprawling into the aisle, books skidding beneath the seats. She grabbed them up as she passed, descended the steps, and clambered up the path to the slow-moving mother; hand slapped away, settling for a fistful of hem. A thumb in her mouth, she turned with a feeble wave.

The image still flickered through Myra's mind as she backed the bus into the cavernous garage, phone wedged beneath her chin—turning the big wheel like an expert croupier—and guided the vehicle between two other buses. "Jilly-Billy, you didn't change your mind, did you?" she said as the line connected.

"Oh, hell no. I'll be there in five—just stopping at the Happy-Mart for a few minis. Apple-Crown, right?"

"Not today," said Myra. "You'd better let me drive."

"Plannin' on it."

As twilight approached, a sepia glare fell over the broad fields of shriveling corn and soybean. The leaves were nearly gone from the surrounding maple, poplar, and boxelder;

sumac, burnt orange and pale, grainy yellow, camouflaged the last stands of dying ash, sentinels, yet to fall. Myra's eyes fell to her companion, face buried in her phone, thumbs working feverishly. "I guess I don't see how you can get so hooked on a kid's game," she said, drumming the steering wheel with her fingers.

"It's harder than you think," said Jill. She paused the game and lit a cigarette. "Was the girl there today?"

"Yeah," said Myra. "Breaks my heart."

"Pretty easy thing when it's hanging off your sleeve." Jill opened her window an inch. "This happens to you every year, you know? You ever stop and talk to one of these kids? Might help."

"No—not really. I wish you could see her."

"She drop her books again?"

"Three days in a row." Myra flicked her brights at an oncoming semi.

Jill stared over at her friend worriedly, dusk shrouding Myra's collapsed features like an Easter Island statue. "Jesus—you gotta let go of that shit," said Jill, rifling through the cellophane of her Pall Mall pack. She touched a roach to the last glow of her cigarette, drew a toke, and offered it across.

Myra waved it away. "You know I can't smoke that shit. Who got it for you this time?"

"Dominic. He came over to fix the door on the trailer," Jill said, returning to the game.

"Who's Domonic, again?"

Jill's head tilted with the screen. "These hang gliders are a bitch to control."

Myra slugged Jill. "Hey—I'm talking here. Domonic, the maintenance guy at the nursing home?"

"He's a good kid—does side jobs—pretty handy," muttered Jill.

"Yeah, I'll bet he's handy," said Myra.

"That's easy for you to say. At least you got Will."

"Yeah—lucky me," said Myra. She peered out at the endless rows of birch, their shadows laying boney fingers across resentful, empty fields. "Haven't heard from him in a week."

"Oh—yes!" exclaimed Jill, raising her phone triumphantly. "Never got past that level before."

"Did you even hear what I said?"

"Buffering —" said Jill, head down, "— yeah, you said something about having Will around to help you keep it warm."

"No—you said that. I said I hadn't seen him in a week."

Jill dropped the phone in her lap. "Oh—sorry," she said in a somber tone. "Is it bad?"

"He's staying up at Ross's deer camp."

"Wait," said Jill, "which Ross we talking about—Carl or Mark? Cause Mark Ross is a total douche, while Carl, on the other hand, is just your average lowlife dirtbag who, for the record, I only slept with once." The tip of Jill's cigarette glimmered like the eye of a rutting buck. "So—Will's hanging with Carl fucking Ross?" she said, smoke rolling from her nostrils. "Guess I figured a man in his forties would've grown out of that whole 'beers and cards and titty bars' phase."

"Growth doesn't appear to be his strong suit."

A half-hour north, the rolling blacktop gave way to crushed rock, the rapidly deteriorating road punctuated by ribs of packed dirt. The rear suspension hopped like a flea-bitten dog as Myra slowed and flicked on the brights. Up the grade, rigid treetops swayed in the wintry breeze, and a red marker flickered amidst slender rods of jack pine; a rusted mailbox mounted on a canoe paddle. They turned in. Maple saplings scraped the underbelly of the SUV as she followed the overgrown two-track to a bowled clearing, the moon dancing off the surface of the twenty-acre lake in the basin. Myra traipsed out to the shed and located the hidden key. Once inside the cabin, she found the fusebox, started the well pump, lit the pilots on the furnace and stove, and the chill crept out of the fisherman's cottage. Myra gathered clean linen and blankets and laid them at the foot of the bed in each bedroom while Jill found a pair of wine glasses.

"I forgot your gramps was a TV star," Jill hollered, a glass of dollar store cabernet sauvignon in hand, skimming over the profusion of photos crowding the walls of the main room. Amid the images of the grey-haired angler showing off trophy fish at a variety of rustic locales were those of a different sort; King Hamlet on the college stage in ghostly armored regalia; live audience television stills, late thirtyish, borderline debonair; awards received at tuxedoed events, a touch of grey at the temples. And on either side of the recliner, a pair of bookcases with odd bits of memorabilia separating time-worn copies of My Side of the Mountain, True Grit, Call of the Wild, Lonesome Dove.

"Not sure star's the right word," said Myra as she came up the hall. "He was a game show host, mostly."

Cut neatly into the windowless wall opposite the big chair was a cupboard. Myra opened both doors. The cedar-lined cabinet was packed with enough puzzles and board games to fill a display case at FAO Schwarz. Jill plucked an oval object from the shelf. "Wooden Brain," she said excitedly. "Let me try this one."

"Hang on, let's box a few of these up first, can we?" In less than an hour, they'd carried a half-dozen cartons to the vehicle. Afterward, Myra rolled her suitcase inside, down the short hall to the main bedroom. When she came out, Jill was at the kitchen table, head tilted sideways, studying the refrigerator door.

"This his game, too?" asked Jill, emptying the wine bottle into her glass.

Myra stole the lit cigarette from the ashtray. "Refrigerator magnets? Not much of a game—he liked to make goofy sentences with them, that's all."

"Sure, but—they're all pressed together in this huge rectangle?" mused Jill.

Myra managed a crooked grin. With a shake of her head, she went out to the mudroom, running her hand along the bamboo pole pinned to the interior wall of the lean-to. Grandpa Gene had taught her to fish off the dock with that pole. Above the window, on the opposite wall, his favorite flyrod and creel, and just below, a pair of Zebco 44's, tips pointing expectantly toward the lake. She opened the screen door and went out to the cleaning station to finish the smoke. The light spilling out from the kitchen caught the hand-carved sign that still hung over the metal bench: 'A fisherman lives here, with the catch of his life.' Grandpa Gene and Grandma Sal always seemed so together, laughing, joking, playing pranks. On one mid-day jaunt to the corner store for ice cream, Grandpa Gene called Sal from the payphone to say they'd caught a bad case of brain freeze and would be late for supper. Myra was eleven then. She turned with a smile. A shadow skittered through the pine needles and down the steep ravine toward the lake; arched-back, a walking bowling ball; a raccoon, perhaps. Myra lifted her phone from her pocket, checking for anything from Will, then put it away and went inside.

"Not sure I ever said—thanks—for helping," said Myra, shaking the chill from her coat. She leaned against the stove.

"I don't mind, hell, wasn't doing anything this weekend, anyhow," said Jill. She examined the fridge and scribbled words onto a notepad.

"No. I mean, for the extra stuff you did for Grandpa— at the nursing home—toward the end. I was glad you were there."

Jill wrote some more. "He grabbed my ass once."

"Grandpa Gene!" said Myra through a brittle laugh. "No frickin' way."

Jill shrugged; a strand of box-dyed blonde bob fell over a puffy eye. "Lots of them old coots grab at you. It's an occupational hazard."

"Well, I wasn't—specifically thanking you for that."

"Never mind. Check this out," said Jill, waving her over. She slid the square pad of paper across the table.

Myra sat down, reading aloud. "The smiling monkey holds the last beat of my heart." Her eyebrows worked together as she stared over at Jill. "What the hell, you're Jim Morrison all of a sudden?"

"No—shithead. Your grandpa's puzzle," said Jill, standing.

Myra scanned the jumble of words stuck to the fridge. "Okay. You want to play? We'll make up a sentence together. I'll start."

Jill raised a hand, "No—wait," gripping the handle of the rust-speckled Coldspot. "The first line. The three words at the top. The pasta lies. What do you think that means?"

"Means you've had a few."

"Nah, c'mon? Take a gander. The pasta lies."

"Who knows? Probably some screwy sentence he was working on. He had all kinds of them. I remember one went something like, 'when fish fly and birds swim, a snake will walk with me to town for supper," Myra said with a snort. "Still gets me."

Jill tottered over and sat down. "You take algebra in school?"

"Hated it. D-minus. Had to go back and get my GED, remember? Took some basic arithmetic, nothing hard. No algebra, that's for sure."

"Thought so." Jill lit a cigarette and waved it back and forth like a smoldering thurible. "Skinny as you are, I know you like Italian food, right? What kind?"

"Nothing fancy. Spaghetti, rigatoni, ravioli, pizza, you name it."

"How about gnocchi?"

"Cute little stuffed noodles? Yeah, I boil a bag of those once in a while. What're you gettin' at?"

"The Pasta Lies," said Jill, drawing deeply, tobacco crackling. "The fibbin' gnocchi. Fibonacci."

"That some kind of pasta sauce?"

"No, stupid, Fibonacci was a mathematician. Take numbers in a line, like one and two. Add the first number to the second number as you go." Jill tugged the paper across the table and wrote it out. "One plus two equals three. Now go back one. Two plus three equals five. Now again. Three and five add up to eight. You just keep going."

Myra tilted her head. "How's a nursing home assistant know that stuff? You use it at work?"

"Oh, hell no. I learned that in high school. One of the few things still with me, shit, twenty-two years later. Where's it go?" Jill pulled a beer can from the fridge, fell back against the door with a smirk. "That's the sentence I came up with when I ran the number sequence left to right across that entire mess of words."

Myra read the page. "The smiling monkey holds the last beat of my heart." She scoured the assorted living room curios, failing to find a monkey, a pith helmet, spear, any jungle-themed object. The man liked to fish.

Jill's phone pinged. She snatched it up excitedly and scurried to the couch. "Fortnite. It's on," she said, stretching out on the cushions, fingers cramped over the keyboard. "Ah, Montague. Back again, you bastard."

Myra grinned, glanced at her wristwatch. "Quarter to twelve," she announced. "I'm going to bed. I'll run to town in the morning for some donuts; you want anything?" Jill's hand popped above the back of the couch, waved her off wordlessly. Exhausted, Myra shuffled down the hall to the main bedroom. She tossed her sweater on the old man's desk and put on her flannel pajamas, listening to Jill in the other room, carping under her breath to her online nemesis. Myra peeled back the covers, sat on the edge of the bed, plucked the bright red twin-bell alarm clock from the nightstand, and sleepily wound the crank, matching time with her watch, setting the alarm for 8:30.

An inch-high face in the middle of the clock grinned back at her: A monkey. Lines creased Myra's tired eyes, the corners of her lips. *Gramps*. A loose fleck of tape on the back of the device scraped her fingernail, and she spun the clock around. "What's this?" she whispered hoarsely, peeling it away, revealing a tiny key. She rolled it in her fingers as an archeologist might a rare amulet, scratched her cheek, probing the room with her eyes. A file cabinet stood in the corner near the closet. The lock didn't budge when she tried it, so she went to the desk. The key opened the bottom drawer. Inside the otherwise empty wooden cube was a slim pocket notebook with obsidian binding, gold-gilded edges, and written on the inside cover in faded, scribbled pencil, a single word: Frances.

***

The following morning, a bleary-eyed Myra sat in her car outside the Early Bird, nibbling on a bear claw. Flecks of glaze fell onto her lap as she flipped open Grandpa's notebook, comparing the hand-drawn sketch inside to the restaurant on the other side of the street: the roofline; the two-story brick structure; the canopy over the patio, a pair of tables beneath; the modest entrance. She'd seen her grandfather tie lures with an artist's precision countless times but never once his drawings. There were two more sketches, done lightly in pencil, both of the same rolling profile: a middle-aged woman, hair piled high, hand on hip, coffee pot in the other, chatting up customers clad in huntsmen garb, a checkerboard draped, window-lined room in the background. The flip-side of one drawing held a short poem:

> *Silence shrouds these*
> *empty years, a foggy morning*
> *lake,*
> *To quiet noiseless stilted*
> *shouts, a new love stirs awake,*
> *A long cast lands alas*
> *too short to lure the one ashore,*
> *A winsome lonesome*
> *shadow, to haunt me evermore.*

A gray sedan came slowly up the road, parked at the curb, and an elderly couple emerged from the vehicle. Myra jogged across the street and followed them into the café. As she slid into the corner booth, a teenaged waitress came around the counter with coffee, stopped to leave a bill on a customer's table, then walked to Myra's. The lanky girl dodged the antler chandelier and laid a menu in front of Myra.

"You already know what you want?" she said emptily, pouring the coffee.

"Got any real cream?"

"Sure," nodded the girl, and she bounded away.

A roaring, boastful laugh broke across the silent room; a pair of older men dressed in quilted flannel shirts and tan khakis. One dropped his fork onto his empty plate and scooted his chair back from the table, rubbing his hand in a circle over his plump stomach. A waitress came through the swinging door, out from the kitchen, hair piled high, a nametag on her chest: Fran.

"Keep it down, Earl, we got customers," Fran scolded in a voice that rattled with the coarseness of a heavy smoker. She wore a modest, knee-length, mustard-colored waitress outfit. Her taperless ankles disappeared into a pair of fat-soled white sneakers that honked against the linoleum as she returned to the kitchen, emerging seconds later with pie. Her foxlike face, clenched, bloodless lips, upturned nose, and dark, darting, close-set eyes held an undefinable appeal that Myra found to be not unpretty.

"Three slices of apple pie for breakfast, holy Jesus," the woman said, banging the plate down in front of Earl. "You get any bigger—you'll have to come in through the service entrance." She slid her forearm over Earl's shoulder as he reached around her waist.

"Yeah, Frannie? How many slices does it take to fuel those battleship hips of yours?" Earl and his friend howled.

"You are what you eat, and you must eat a lot of shrimp," Fran fired back. "Now tell me, what'd ya bag today, sweetie?"

Earl tugged her close. "Nothin'. Already filled our tags. We just like bein' out there, chasin' game."

"You're gamey alright—whew!" barked Fran, pinching her nose. She pried herself from his grip and tapped the younger waitress on the arm as she passed. "Hey, Heather, stayin' late today, right?"

"Yeah, yeah, I remember. You're workin' a split," the girl said, delivering the mini-pitcher of cream to Myra. "But you gotta be back by four like you promised. I ain't workin' breakfast, lunch, and dinner."

Fran leaned into Earl's ear. "She always bitchy when it's her time," she said, loud enough for the room to hear. She waddled into the kitchen, cackling to herself.

A half-hour later, from her car outside the restaurant, Myra waited for Fran to climb into a rusted sedan, then followed her to the northern edge of the two-blinker-light town. The woman parked behind a two-story brick building.

Myra coasted past and wheeled around, returning in time to catch a glimpse of Fran traipsing up the alley, ducking through an ash-colored steel door with stick-on letters, Sully's aligned crookedly across the face. She parked at the back of the crumbling lot and walked around to the front entrance. The nearly deserted tavern reeked of damp wood, stale beer, and cheap soap. At the end of the 20-foot mahogany bar sat an old man, hovering over a glass of beer as if landing a spacecraft, muttering incoherently into the bartender's ear, who was bent over washing glasses. They both turned as Myra lost her footing along the uneven floor. She caught herself on a wobbly stool, leaned against the counter, searching the dimly lit pub for Frances. The bartender drew up from the sink, wiping his hands with an apron, a look of blank regard ironed onto his pasty face. His uncombed hair grew in patches like weeds alongside a gully, and he edged nearer with the strained politeness of someone late for a cigarette.

"What'll it be."

"I—uh," said Myra, pawing through her purse for nothing in particular.

The man checked the clock. "We don't serve lunch for another hour."

The floorboards creaked over Myra's head, dust fell from the ceiling. She heard a woman's muffled voice, talking, laughing. "Coffee," said Myra.

"Have to make a fresh pot, only be a minute." He flicked on the coffeemaker, filled the pot, and disappeared into the backroom.

The codger at the end of the bar raised his head and spun away from the counter, spidery elbows flaring. He rose from the stool and tottered past the jukebox to the restroom. At the end of the long hallway, partially lit by an exit sign, a pair of heavy boots clomped slowly down the staircase. A large man came up the hall, tucking a loose shirttail into his waistband. "Gotta pick up a load out in Oregon," he said, "taking a haul to St. Louis." He stopped at the lip of the barroom to tighten his belt.

A woman's voice echoed up the hallway. "So—a couple of weeks, then." Fran edged her way past, slapped his rump, and scooted into the barroom, a pair of fleshy thighs in skin-tight jeans, hair tousled loosely over her shoulders, cheeks dotted with rouge, a hazy blur of perfume and cosmetics that failed to negate her untamed, granite surface.

Myra grabbed a sugar packet from the bartop dispenser and gave it a shake, pretending to watch the steam rise from the coffee pot.

Fran pried her phone from her back pocket and slid into a barstool. Her glued-on fingernails flicked mindlessly at the pink, rhinestone-covered device, then it thrummed alive with a pulsing disco beat in her palm. "Yeah? Hey—right, sure," she said, hopping down from the stool, zigzagging between the empty tables, twirling her hair with her finger. "Oh, yeah? Sounds good. Anytime before one's okay. Yep—Sully's, on Main. Park in the back." She returned to the bar, and like a twitchy old hen, nestled delicately onto the stool.

A pan rattled in the kitchen. "Drew?" Fran huffed. She pulled a cigarette from her purse, tapped it on the bar. "Who the hell you gotta screw around here to get a beer?" She blew a cloud of smoke at the tin ceiling, then pounded down the hallway in her low heels, stopped for one final drag, and flicked the butt outside. "Drew!" she shouted again on the way back. The kitchen door swung open, and the bartender poked his head through. Fran tapped her shoe on the floor. "Can I get a draft?" she said, pointing to her chair.

A knot formed in Myra's chest. Could this really be the last person to stir Grandpa Gene's heart? Drew delivered her coffee and a beer for Fran. As he returned to the kitchen, Fran raised a toast across the elbow of the bar, one eye closed, a stout finger aimed at Myra.

"You were up at the Early Bird this morning."

"Yeah."

"Thought so." The woman drank deeply from her glass.

Myra twirled a spoon in her cup. "You been working up there long?"

"Seventeen years. Can't say I ever saw you there, sweetie." Fran glared across. "You a cop?"

"School bus driver—if you can believe it." Myra glanced around, chuckling softly to herself. "Off duty."

"Hah," said the woman, slapping the bartop, "that's rich. No such thing as off-duty, if you ask me."

"You live here?"

Fran followed Myra's eyes to the ceiling. "For the time being."

"Boyfriend's on the road a lot?" said Myra.

Fran took another swallow and wiped the froth from her lip. "You might say that. How about you? Married, right?"

Myra shook her head. "Was, for a couple of years. He left me for a librarian. They got two kids now."

"He was probably sleeping around. They all do."

"Pretty sure he was." Myra wiped her nose with her sleeve. "After the divorce, he told me that driving a school bus was a job in which I was doomed to flourish. Me and my eggless womb."

Jagged red lines flared in Fran's eyes. "Sounds like a first-class prick."

Myra sipped her coffee and shook her head. The woman had said what she was thinking, though it seemed she had no right to say it. "I hope this isn't too forward," said Myra, the words spilling out uneasily, "But I'm up here— cleaning my grandpa's fishing cabin. And I came across these." She removed the old man's drawings from her jacket pocket and slid them over.

"Oh," Fran said slowly, palm against her cheek, eyes darting between the two sketches. "There's a—" she stood up and laid the pages on the bar "—The resemblance is—who did these? You say your grandad?" She peered hungrily toward the door and tugged her jeans into place. "Is he out there, waitin', or something?"

Myra was about to explain as Drew walked up, a slip of paper flopping between his fingers. "Yo-Francis," he said and laid it on the counter in front of her. "Tab and rent. Due Monday." He knelt down to load a case of beer into the refrigerator.

An oak leaf skipped up the hallway on a breeze, crossing the floor to nestle next to the jukebox. The rear door of the bar banged shut. A man's voice shouted, "Frannie! You up there?" Stair treads creaked as he lumbered up to the second floor. Drew vanished into the kitchen. Frances fished her lipstick from her purse, drew on a smile, then waddled down the hall, beer in hand, whistling.

On the way back to Gene's cabin, Myra's mind churned with disbelief, each thought freighted with remorse, forgotten lovers, destiny's wheel. Had her mannerly grandfather somehow been interested in that moth-eaten, hash-slinging harlot? And if so, what would her own prospects hold? Could she love, in whatever form it might take? She might end up alone, a spinster or worse, like Frances, if she really was *the* Frances. Was it wrong of Gene to desire one last indulgence, of his own free will? His big, beautiful, burning heart, overflowing with loss, dying from lament. Still brooding as she neared the cabin, Myra wheeled the car along the marsh-flanked road, willow branches swishing the sides like pen strokes, in search of some quiet comfort, a place where the long-grieving widower might be forgiven for having one final fling.

***

Fall's winds carry fresh hope, a new harvest. Even after seventeen years as a school bus driver. *Today would be different*, thought Myra, as the spindly, close-mouthed girl vaulted onto the bus that Monday morning, a perky brown-eyed Susan stuck like a teddy bear's nose behind her ear, a wad of them in her sweaty fist. With a lifeless smile, chin to her chest, the girl passed the flowers to Myra, then in a wordless dash, found her spot, four rows back. She stared out with anxious breaths, wiping away the oval of fog from the window in time to see the purple-sunflower muumuu dissolve into the overgrown path. As the bus rumbled up to a stop sign, Myra's eyes went to the mirror and caught the child looking back, a dash of crimson on her cheeks. She reached for the small wax-coated bag next to her lunchbox, pulled it to her lap, and wondered if the girl might like to share a donut.

Selected Poems by David C. Hall

A literary conversation

"That fuckin' guy," he says,
my friend Alec that is,
drinking stout,
which is so black
it looks like food
and is
in all its thick and mysterious blackness
a kind of nourishment.

"That fuckin' guy," he says again,
referring to someone we both know
but do not like that much
and who now enjoys a certain success.

And I just nod
drinking my stout.
The first swallow,
that's the best,
when you feel the world
opening up before you
in all its beauty
and immensity,
and as you get down
to the bottom of the pint
in all its foamy blackness
a gentleness washes over you,

and you remember once again
how the consumer society
is crap, how
it's the simple things that count,

this stout for instance,
earth and river
in its blackness.

"No technique, no nuance,
all fuck and shit
and cunt and bitch.
Anybody can do that."

"So why didn't you?" I ask him.
Maybe it's the beer that's got to me now
or I'm just sick of all his moaning.

"Well, he got there first,
didn't he?" he says,
my friend Alec.
"That fuckin' guy."

When the barbarians come

The barbarians came down

out of the hills again last night,

kicked in the door and hanged the dog

and stole my entire collection

of glass elephants,

smashing mother's precious china,

drinking our whiskey

as I lay out there

on the hard cold ground

beneath the plaster Cupid,

clenched my teeth.

And how they laughed!

"Next time we will be ready,"

I muttered later,

sweeping up the broken glass.

"Next time we will be ready."

But then that's what we always say.

The old woman in the wheelchair

The old woman in the wheelchair bought a small bottle of
wine in the airport cafe.
Once she had liked red wine, though it seemed a long time
since she had tasted wine of any kind.
Soon the little bottle was empty. She would have liked some
more but fell asleep instead.
"What flight are you on, ma'am?" A voice said.
A young man in a blue uniform, a young man with a bright,
kindly face and bushy brown eyebrows.
Even his breath smelled clean.
Earlier she had seen him talking to a blonde girl, also in a blue
uniform.
They laughed and smiled when they talked together and
moved their hands in graceful, expressive gestures when
attending to anxious and uncertain passengers.

They were happy in their work, they were happy in their bodies.

All around the old woman people ate and drank and moved their mouths as they chewed and spoke, poked at their cell phones and tore open packages of potato chips with their teeth. The old woman in the wheelchair wondered for a moment

who had brought her here and where she was meant to go.

Selected Poems by Jean Harper

Revision

When Dad was still alive our Magnolia tree – the one by the highway – blossomed. For a week in February, Indiana felt warm, like May or June or ordinary summer. Then, winter again. The new flowers just died, pink skins burnt black.

The day my father dies, my sister sends my brother an email and copies it to me. "Dad," she writes, "will be buried in his grey suit with the subtle pinstripes, a white shirt, his good black dress shoes, and a red tie with blue dots."

Long ago, when my father was impossibly young and I

was ten, my sister was a baby. I used to change her diapers. Once, I stuck her tiny bum with a diaper pin.

It slid in deep. It was an accident. It only happened once.

"Yesterday," she writes, "I got Dad to help with the tie. A few of the ones he used to wear looked good with the suit, so I bunched those up like a bouquet, and told Dad to pick one. He chose well – he will look very spiffy."

Semis long as strip malls roar past our house. They scatter dead Magnolia petals. A red tie nudges my father's hand.

Long ago a diaper pin punctured pink flesh. I stared and stared.

The tiny baby is so pale, so hairless, shrieking. I do it again.

Errands

We were in your blue station wagon –
heading to the supermarket for chicken – or maybe fish –

then the Post Office to mail the bills –
and the cleaners to retrieve Dad's pressed shirts.

Before anything we pulled in and stopped
at the Esso filling station. Your car rolled over the cord,

tripped the bell and the attendant materialized.
You lowered your window. "Fill it up, please."

He did what you asked, turning between gas pump
and our long car with the grace of a dancer –

you watched him and I watched you. That day,
instead of just one we got two Tiger drinking glasses.

We drove away into the rest of the afternoon
and then you said –

do you remember this –
          you said:

"Sometimes I would just like to chuck it – all of it –
and run away – with someone, anyone."

You kept your hands on the steering wheel – I held
the Tiger glasses – the gray road unfurling silently before us.

Selected Poems by Emily Wagner

What the Dog Said

My husband and his good friend often go hiking. That is, in fact, what they do. They talk about good food, good drink, good music, and life, lengthening their strides and taking in the views. Of course, sometimes they do encounter others. I imagine them, like Frost and his walking friend Edward Thomas, alone in a desolate wood, perhaps facing a fork in the road, laughing heartily, and easily taking the road they have never taken, no poetic consultation required here. As usual, when my husband arrives home, weary, sweated, and smiling, he relays to me the day's adventure. On one such recent walking occasion, my husband and his friend encountered two trail runners and their dog. *Today is hill intervals day*, the man said pointing up the hill, eyes wide, breath labored, running in place as he talked to ensure no calories lost. As my husband shared this story with me, I thought of Jack London's prospector and his dog, the poor native husky, stuck with an arrogant man, trying by sundown to get back to camp with the boys. In London's story the dog gives the man numerous signs, his instincts much truer than the man's judgment. Still, only the husky survives, while the chechaquo, who ignored everyone's advice, and tried to create one last bit of warmth by attempting to kill the husky, failed, and then ran around in the snow like a chicken with his head cut off, before collapsing from the inwardly expanding freeze. This is how London describes it. The man, as we know, dies alone in the Klondike snow while the husky trots on to safety. This dog, my husband encountered was similar in its wisdom, though much more domestic than London's version, and perhaps wiser for having dealt longer with humans. He immediately took action. He stopped and sniffed the food my husband and his friend had packed, he lingered especially near the bologna,

tongue hanging out, and there remembered *conserving* energy should always be his goal. He sat down abruptly, stretched and leaned way back, propped his rear paws on a nearby timber, and pulled out a pipe he had tucked between his collar and his fur. *Aren't you going to rejoin your friends?* my husband asked. By this time the dog had lit his pipe and was grinning widely, as we all know dogs can do, *Ah, what's the use?* he said as he puffed and scratched vigorously behind his left ear. *I don't think they're here for my sake*, the dog continued. *You know what I think?* he said leaning forward, *I think they're just running around the forest, looking down,*
and trying not to fall.

Iowa

I never thought of it as a threat
until we were there in the middle of the night
in the rising unstable air of a summer storm
that seemed about to funnel up.
We were just young enough to be moving
across the Iowa plains at 2 a.m.
and just old enough to feel the fear of things unexpected,
bodies across open space, and limits.
Still, there we were in our minivan on the open highway.
That night wind and rain battered the broad barrenness
and us, the only friction in its path,
swiftly forced off the road to wait it out,
not a single other headlight in sight.
Iowa's green and red presence and gentle calling name
never did feel soft to me again after that night.
Something like the wild potential of nature
to pull us back down to where we belong,
to call us back from swaying and daydreaming.
Derecho was what they called it,

and it was, in fact, direct and straight, but it felt
like a vengeful forgotten nephilim traveling eastward,
barreling through us on a quest
for woods, water, or some firm place to land.
We made it to Wyoming before we stopped again,
but the spell had already been cast,
and our nerves and exhaustion produced illusory results,
for Iowa was, after all, just an open space
we traveled through,
not a fiendish foreign god bent on destruction
or delaying our delight.
Yet, it wasn't until Montana that its grip finally fell
and we could take in the liberating sunshine
without remembering the soak of rain
and we could feel the dry breeze
without fearing the wind.

The Passage of Time

I.   It shook us awake in our twenties; one violent tug and
     we nearly lost our footing. Still, our paths remained
     many, always beginning bold and abundant and ending
     in dust and longing, a barren flat which opened and
     quickly closed. As we rounded the corner into our
     thirties, its loitering was ever present, always pointing
     us to the vacant spot at the end of the row, both dimly
     lit and beckoning. Uneasiness and grizzle patterned our
     days. Then an invisible force found us. It fixed our
     faces in front of an infinitely growing hourglass, a firm
     hand gripping the back of our necks, feeling more like
     mercy than pain, and so we folded our hands before it.
     When we could not move no matter our method and

we saw that the hourglass quickened as it went, the sand falling at an increasing speed, mounding up swiftly inside, we moved and peered in closer, our faces pushing near the glass, wondering why it appeared to have changed.

II.   At last we finally back away and loosen ourselves, putting an end to the firm hold we had on our lives, for we realize now, after all, that the whole train is moving too fast for us and we'll never be able to take it all in or keep up. We release the strings from our glistening desires, sending them drifting up over the rooftops and out of sight. Striving and ambition flicker out and we press them gently underfoot. Now the speed increases with such intensity and rapidity that we do lose our balance and fall flat on our backs, but from the ground looking up at the sky, things are enchanting and far better than we could have ever expected. The birds sing and we take them in, guessing their names by the trill in their voices and their cadence. With each cloud comes calm and wonder at the particles and places piling up under the sun that we will never see. Small voices with laughter like the trickle of a mountain spring we drink from all day long bring a holy warmth and wetten our eyes so that we almost get up to wipe them, but then just as quickly their little feet form vibrations that hold us down, their weight heavy and pressing. This part of our life, we realize, will be spent pinned down and intoxicated. And so we stay on our backs, waving our hands at all the passersby. We smile up at them, trying to coax them down to listen and feel the tiny vibrations that we feel and all the coolness and easy breathing that comes with lying this low. At night we dream of Heaven, with its open door at the foot of the mountain and the sound and sparkle of its gilded mandolins.

How to Thanksgiving
By Tal Corvus

Wake before the sun
　this is not hard
Collect the ashes
　　from the fires that have
　　warmed your family over the months
The year
　　put them in a barrel
　place sticks of wood, one
　　at a time on top
of the ashes

Try to recall
　　all of your joys and sorrows
　　since the last time, until
　　you have a pile
Light this pile on fire

Collect your family
　　your friends, at the last minute
　　if you have to
Say please

Place the body of what once
　　was living over the fire
Stand around, worrying
about where you may have gone wrong
　　add sugar
　　add wood
Make promises to the bodies
　　you are caring
　　for, you are all trying to sustain
One another

As soon as the fire is done
   with the flesh
the moment you have snapped
   at your auntie
Gather around the table
   the places the children have set
say something that begins
   to get at how happy you are
to have these bodies
to hold you up
to watch burn
   with the light of stars
flung through space
Trajectories unknown.

The Rounding Errors
By Aurin Shaila Nusrat Sheyck

If our stories are algorithms,
Today is
The rounding error.
Present leaning on past choices,
And all the rounding errors added up to make this moment
All those choices brought you here—
Here, now, this place, this room,
this salmon color of your wall, this loveseat you are sitting on,
the scars on your back.

I ignored the decimal places,
rounding up
rounding down
not to overcomplicate my story
But,
One more decimal place for all the choices,
might be living on the next street
In a house with backyard stretching to the Pine woods,
No doors with broken hinges
no anger issues
maybe less back pain
from all the liftings,
Or no liftings at all.

One more decimal place for the first smoke,
The ride from the steamy neighbor,
the birthday party,
the untaken country trip
the hung-up calls and the not calling-backs

One more decimal place for the choice of
whether to attend business school,
giving up after rejections,

more giving ups,
and not many letting go-s

But I wonder if the Pine woods would still be there
And In the woods, the shining ponds like the mysterious eyes
of
An old lady
With a crooked stick and white frizz.

Shining under the steamy white sun.

I took a walk to the woods.

Selected Poems by Rachael Inciarte

say that I am

one of those
full moon women
a swallowed the star, hot bellied
      wicked in white
      women

I am that type the
look
while you leap
women winged
      mid flight
      monster women
the kind whose shadow
shifts shape
beneath them

I am one
the search your myths well
women

      true
even my falls
find finer footing
      true
fruit that would spoil
remains ripe on my vine

I am one of those
witch women,
      cursed
      where I stand and
      refusing to burn

sex ed.
[altered nonet]

they taught us the birds and bees but we
learned for ourselves that flesh means flower / how
thorns hide among petals / and that nectar
is dangerous for what it feeds /
take care where you plant
seeds / they may grow /

where do babies
come from?
fuck.

in case of emergency

sometimes I fantasize fires
and sometimes floods

think sea waters rising
sweeping away cities, sinking suburbs
imagine
we climb the stairs
cut holes into the ceiling
wait on the roof to be rescued
our arms are exhausted flags but
we drown
when help doesn't come

I've scripted years worth of disasters
earthquakes, blackouts, and invasions
I am safe from nothing and no one
survives

isn't that why we are always signing
in case of emergency ?
because these things can happen

what if? I wonder
what then?

Revision
By Cassady O'Reilly-Hahn

Leaf: a draft
the tree hates.
Crumpled pages
tossed to soil.
Ten-thousand revisions
on my fucking lawn.

Totality
By Laura Keller

Joss didn't see me, but I saw him.

It was the day the sun was going to disappear, but in that moment, I wanted to disappear. Boredom had brought me into the old antique shop—*Grandma's Attic*—in Sedalia, Missouri where my dad had schemed our viewing of the eclipse. It'd taken us two hours to get there from Kansas City, and after setting up our chairs and getting his clunky telescope and camera put together, I'd just needed a break from ... well, from Dad.

"Set your timer, Chloe," he'd said when I asked if I could go look around. "Be back in fifteen minutes. That'll give plenty of time before the eclipse starts. You don't want to miss anything."

In an exaggerated display of obedience, I pulled my phone out and set the timer, holding it up as proof.

He nodded, approving. "You're gonna love this. Better than an *epic rager*."

Lately my dad had this cringeworthy habit of peppering our conversations with teen speak. I had to give him credit for trying. He had a lot to juggle these days, including relating to his teen daughter as a newly-single parent.

"Right. Epic rager. Got it."

The historic town center of Sedalia was pretty much how you'd expect an old town square to look. City Hall in the middle, where we'd set up, surrounded by mom and pop shops along the periphery. We'd officially entered a small-town cliché.

But now, as I hovered over a bowl of antique keys, Joss Gibson stood a mere two aisles away in a shop only slightly more organized than an episode of *Hoarders*, layering in another cliché: junior class stoner meets up with class overachiever. He stood by a glass counter displaying dead critter skulls, bugs mounted in paperweights, and poisonous snakes frozen in mid-hiss.

I dropped the dreamy vintage key I'd discovered back into the bowl so I could make a swift exit. Except it *plinked* when it landed, and Joss lifted his head.

Dammit. Eye contact.

Joss gave a chin nod, then wandered my direction, looking ever-disheveled, yet absolutely comfortable in his own skin.

"Eclipse?" he asked. He dove a hand into the vat of keys and swished around.

"Yep." Why had he come over? Back at school we would have passed in the hall without a glance. I couldn't stand the silence he seemed super-chill with, so I blurted out, "Come here often?" before I could process how lame it would sound.

Joss nodded—which had to be a bunch of crap, because we were hours from school in an antique store for Pete's sake.

"I was joking," I said.

"I caught that. But, I do know this place."

"Riiight." I checked my phone. Three minutes left.

"You don't believe me?"

I squinted my eyes at him. Did he seriously think I was that gullible?

"I'll prove it." With nothing more than a side-nod, he strolled ahead with full confidence that I'd follow—which, admittedly, I did. I kinda wanted to call him out on his bullshit.

He veered down an adjacent aisle and pointed to an old-fashioned suitcase resting flat on a faded blue end table. "Best part of the whole shop. Right there." Joss stood tall, chest raised, arms crossed, somehow looking serious despite his just-rolled-out-of-bed head.

I nodded, not knowing how to respond. It was a ratty looking suitcase.

"Open it," he challenged.

"Um. No thank you."

He feigned heartache with a hand to his chest. "Such trust issues."

I shrugged my shoulders. Having your mom suddenly bail on your family will do that.

"Fine, I'll do it," he said. He reached down and popped the suitcase open. I braced myself for something ultra-bizarre, but instead it held a collection of yellowed vintage photos. Chock full. And for some reason, they hit me hard. So many memories, boxed up and forgotten.

"Check it out." He lifted an old photo perfectly capturing the glint in a young woman's eye as she looked at someone off-camera.

I held out my hand, and Joss passed it to me. The woman in the picture was so full of life, caught there in a single moment in time. Forever. She suddenly didn't seem so forgotten. She seemed ... well-remembered.

"Very cool," I said. And for the first time all day, my words matched how I felt.

Joss reached into the suitcase for more, and I allowed my hand to follow his, slipping another photo in my fingers.

Then my *By the Seaside* tone piped in. My time was up. A twinge of regret rattled my ribs.

"I gotta go."

Joss motioned to my phone. "Is that an eclipse countdown?" I couldn't tell if he was making fun of it, or just curious or what. Might as well confess what a dork I was.

"Yeah. I'm kinda supposed to get out there with my dad or he's going to have a heart attack."

"Okay." He shut the suitcase and a cloud of dust rose into the air. "Let's go."

Wait, what?

"We can't miss this thing. Last time it happened around here was in the 1800s."

So, Joss was interested—and knowledgeable—about the science-geek event of the year?

He wove his way to the front door, but this time he glanced back to make sure I was following him—which I was—and waved, shouting, "See ya, Stan!" The bell on the door announced our departure, like we were about to end scene.

Holy crap. Joss really *did* know the shop owner. That wasn't bullshit? But the bigger looming question at hand: was Joss coming with me to meet my dad?

Joss, with the not-so-subtle scent of pot emanating from his torn-up t-shirt, was definitely not who Dad had planned to watch the eclipse with. Or who Dad would want me hanging with. At all.

"So, are you here with someone?" It flowed out of me, like lava bubbling from my anxious volcano-mouth.

But Joss only shrugged as we crossed the street together. "I've got family in town, but today I'm calling my own shots."

"Um. Okay."

We headed toward the spot my dad and I'd set up. I could easily pick him out in the crowd, proudly wearing his "Eclipse 2017 ... TOTALITY Cool" t-shirt. He was scanning the area for me with his dad-radar.

From my vantage point, looking in on *our spot*, I suddenly realized how empty our space was. How one missing person could make it look like a crater had formed right in front of you. We'd planned this outing together—the three of us—over a year ago. Things change.

Dad finally saw me and waved me over. Enthusiastically.

"That," Joss said, "must be your dad."

"Um, yeah." I threw on my fake smile. "He's pretty excited about this whole thing."

"It's all good," Joss said, pulling eclipse glasses out of his pocket and flashing them around like they were a prize. "It's a big fucking deal. Full totality."

"I guess." I really didn't care about the totality—the sun being completely blocked out vs. seeing most of it blocked. You had to use protective glasses either way—just with totality you had like a minute (well, in our case exactly one minute and twenty-nine seconds, my dad had informed me) where you could shed the glasses and look directly at the sun while it was fully blocked out. Whoopee.

"So, it's just you and your dad?" Joss asked, the way only Joss Gibson would. Without giving a crap about what his question might be digging at.

"Yep."

We walked in silence 'til we almost got to my dad, then Joss reached out and quick-tapped my shoulder. A good-bye pat. "Hey, I better go."

"Yeah, okay." And just like that, Joss veered left where I went right. And I wanted to be fine with that—with us parting ways and moving on with our lives.

But I had this tugging feeling, a tiny string pulling at this invisible part of me that cared about things. The part of me that'd wanted to stay and sift through more pictures together in *Grandma's Attic*.

"Joss, wait—," I called out. "Do you want to watch the eclipse? With us?"

He stopped abruptly and turned back, and for a moment I thought he might say yes.

"I'm good. I've ... got a thing. But, enjoy the show." He left me with the same wave he'd given Stan back at the shop.

I drew in a deep breath, wishing myself away from Joss and Sedalia and that stupid eclipse. Why had I let myself ask him that?

Oh well. At least now I didn't need to worry about him dropping f-bombs around my dad, or lighting up as the eclipse reached totality.

"Who was that?" Dad asked as I walked up. He was squinting in Joss's direction, probably analyzing how much of a troublemaker he was.

"Oh, just a kid from school."

"Well, you better go catch him."

"What?"

"Those eclipse glasses he was holding ... they're the ones that were recalled. He could seriously damage his retinas."

He had to be kidding. "For real?"

"Scout's honor." His nerdy three finger pledge confirmed it. "You need to tell him. I couldn't live with myself if a kid was blinded on the best day of the year."

Best day of the year? Our family had been broken apart only two months ago. This year could never have a best anything.

"Either you go, or I will," he said.

I closed my eyes, trying to visualize which scenario was worse. Approaching Joss after his stiff rejection sounded about as lovely as vomiting. But, the thought of having Dad go all fatherly on him was beyond mortifying.

"Fine," I huffed.

Dad shuffled through our back pack, retrieving the other pair of protective glasses. "Here."

Seeing them stole my breath.

I offered a hesitant hand, and Dad pinched the glasses a moment too long when I went to take them.

Dammit, Mom. How was it that she kept reappearing when she wasn't even there?

With glasses in hand, I headed back to where I'd come from like I was walking through honey. Thick and slow and very, very sticky.

I found Joss sidled up in a food line that looked to be some potluck picnic set up on the square. A church function I

hadn't noticed when we first set up. But now it was obvious—
the Salvation Singers were belting out *hallelujah* off to the
side, and the Praise Craze Puppet Show was set up on the
opposite corner. Somehow we'd landed in a church gathering
on the town square. Perfect.

And there was Joss Gibson, church crasher. I
swallowed against the lump forming in my throat and
reminded myself to breathe. Then I sucked it up and walked
over.

"I didn't peg you for the churchgoing type," I said.

He turned to me and double-blinked before his face
settled back into chill Joss mode. "Church? Me? *Hell* no. I'm
just in it for the food." He swept his hand over the spread.
"Want some?"

"You're inviting me to this food line you're mooching
from?"

"Sure. Don't wanna be rude." He winked, and I'm not
sure if it was intentional or not, but either way, that was all it
took. Something in me suddenly *got* Joss Gibson.

He wasn't someone who never gave a crap about
anything. He was someone who only gave a crap about things
he really cared about.

What would that would feel like? To shed all the expectations of everyone around you? How nice would that be just to care about what really mattered in the here and now?

Joss proceeded to load up his plate with lumps of potato salad and greasy fried chicken.

"I have bad news," I announced. "*And* good news."

"Okay," he said, unfazed, moving on to the sweet tea. "Lay it on me."

I broke the news about the glasses. Joss's whole face fell, and suddenly I could see what he must've looked like as a little boy. Dammit. I might've only had one parent represented there, but at least I had one—one who was looking out for me. Where were Joss's parents? Why hadn't they cared that his eyes might fry?

"Well, I'm out of luck," he said. "Looks like I'll be zapping my eyeballs, because I'm not missing this thing." He sighed, trying to balance his plate and tea while reaching for a napkin and fork, but then his chicken slid off his plate onto the ground.

"Shit."

"Here, let me help you," I said.

"No, forget it." He chucked his whole plate into a nearby garbage can out of frustration.

"Hey, at least you still have your sweet tea," I said.

"Right. Great."

"And also ... there's these." I waved the glasses in front of him. "I told you there was good news."

"What? No, I can't take yours."

"It's okay. They're spares." I had a hard time saying it out loud.

"Really? Holy hell." He took the glasses, with humble appreciation in his eyes. "Thanks. Someday I'll get my shit together."

"It's no big deal," I said.

"It kinda is."

Suddenly, a preacher from the church began booming over a megaphone. "This eclipse is God showing us a sign ... to awaken us ... to remind us of our sins. We must repent before it's too late!"

Joss and I burst out laughing. What kind of doomsday scenario had we stumbled into?

"Anything you'd like to confess?" he asked.

The challenge in his tone made me want to confess to something legit. Failing to book our speaker for the Future Entrepreneurs Club wouldn't quite cut it. I knew what I needed to say.

"Those glasses were my mom's."

Joss swallowed some tea in a hard gulp. "What?"

"She left us. Took off. Gone." I'd never shot it straight like that before. I'd always made it sound like *my parents grew apart*, or *it was best for everyone*. What a bunch of crap.

"Oh, shit." Joss's eyes fluttered to the lawn, a silent apology.

"Yeah. It sucks." She'd chosen someone else. Squashed my dad's heart. Mine too. "I kinda hate her for it."

"Well, now there you go. That's a proper confession." Joss raised his cup into the air, like a toast, and yelled, "Here's to shitty moms everywhere!"

I laughed, and smiled from somewhere deep. From somewhere that was authentically me.

The Salvation Singers went back to their music. Joss and I shared another smirk, then sank into awkwardness as we stood in limbo.

"Well, I should get back with my dad for the eclipse." I wanted to be the one to break it up this time.

Joss took one last swig of tea. "I'll come with you."

The surprise must have shown on my face.

"I mean," Joss stammered, "if the offer still stands. It'd be cool. You know, to watch it with you. And plus, you saved my vision and everything."

My insides went mush and I dug down to remember how to speak. "Sure. Let's ... we'd better ..."

"Yeah, let's go."

Between the minister's latest warning about the occult, Joss and I together in that strange alternate universe, and the fact that the sun was about to go dark, it felt like some kind of mind-blowing apocalypse really was in motion.

"Check it out. It's started." Joss pointed to crescent-shaped slivers of leaf shadows on the sidewalk. He brought his glasses to his face and looked up at the sun. "Look," he said.

I put my glasses on. A sliver of the sun was missing. It actually did look kinda neat.

"It'll get better," Joss said. "The solar corona's gonna be killer. We'll see it with our bare eyes."

"Okay, between attending a church picnic and spouting off astronomy facts, you're shaking my worldview here. How do you know so much about this?" I asked.

Joss laughed, but then his face turned serious. "My grandma. She saw a total eclipse once. Told me stories about it that sounded like magic. When I was younger, and my grandma was taking care of me while my parents tried to get their shit together—which they still haven't done, by the way—she took me to watch an annular eclipse. Kinda like this one, but we couldn't take the glasses off. But today, we get to see the total eclipse through our own eyes. That's the magic."

The thought of little Joss and his grandma looking out at the open sky together and finding such wonder was about the sweetest image I could conjure up.

We finally made it back to my dad, and while I was relieved he didn't have a lecture waiting for me about how I'd missed the beginning of the eclipse, I was bummed that our timing had cut Joss off from sharing more about his grandma. I liked the way his face lit up when he talked about her.

Dad was more relaxed about having Joss join us than I expected. Mostly he was just thankful that Joss had heeded our warning not to fry his eye sockets. And, if I'm being honest, I think we both felt a little more complete with an extra person there.

"Did you see it's started?" Dad asked, seeping enthusiasm. He had us look through his telescope. Over a quarter of the sun had vanished.

"Awesome," I said. And I did mean it, but for some reason I preferred seeing it with my own eyes—even with glasses—instead of looking through a machine.

"Just you wait," he said. "Prepare to be amazed."

Dad and I only had two chairs, so there was this weird pause where we figured out who would sit where. Eventually Joss and I took a seat on the blanket and left one chair empty next to my dad. It kinda hurt to look at, but Dad would be tinkering with his camera during the eclipse anyway, so I figured he'd be okay.

"So, shouldn't you be watching this with your grandma?" I asked Joss a while after we'd gotten settled. A half second later, I realized we were both missing someone that day. It was his turn to confess.

"We had a plan to watch it together—my grandma and me. This is where she lived. That shop we were at ... that's where my folks sold her stuff."

"So, she's gone," I confirmed.

"Right after Thanksgiving. Pneumonia, the bastard."

"I'm really sorry."

He waved it off, trying to be all Joss about it. "My parents don't give a damn about any of this," he said, reaching up to the sky like he wanted to hug it. "And, my friends would give me a load of shit for caring so much. So, I decided to come down here on my own today and catch it."

"Well, it's kinda like being with your grandma. In spirit," I said, seeing him in a whole new way. Right then, that image—of Joss sitting in the town square, looking up at the sky, connecting with his grandma—surpassed the earlier image I'd had of him as a kid.

"Look, kids! It's getting close." Dad chimed in, cutting a slice through the world that Joss and I'd inhabited the past few minutes, bringing me back into the current one which was rapidly darkening. I had a sudden awareness of how much cooler it had gotten. How the mugginess had dropped off. How good the breeze felt playing with my hair.

I peered through my glasses again. Over half the sun had disappeared, and a genuine flutter of interest raced through me. It was strangely satisfying to witness a section of the sun go missing.

The minister piped in again over his megaphone— something about a chance at redemption—and while Dad busied himself with his telescope, Joss looked over at me, and lowered his glasses.

"Check it out," he said, nodding at the streetlamps that had just flickered on. It was like night, but not night. A different kind of darkness. A beautiful darkness I'd never witnessed before.

Maybe it wasn't the worst thing for the sun to go dark every once and while. There could be beauty in dark. I was looking right at it.

Joss Gibson. Bad boy. Wrong boy. And there in Sedalia, Missouri, on the day of that eclipse, he shined. Why did it take the dark to make me see him in this light? I wasn't Miss Priss and he wasn't Stoner Boy. We were just two kids in the sudden cool and dark of the summer, on some other planet together witnessing the end of the world as we knew it. Or maybe the beginning of a new world. One that would last for one minute and twenty-nine seconds.

The sliver got smaller and smaller. The sky darkened and the cicadas buzzed. The choir quieted. The puppetry stopped. Even the minister went silent, and we all just watched. All of us on that square, together. One humanity, collectively watching our sun disappear right in front of us. Letting that void fill us up.

And it was absolutely unstoppable—bigger than myself, or Joss, or my dad. I felt like an ant. No, like ... dust? It was such a relief to feel so small. To know life was so much larger than me. Larger than a mom who ditched you or a grandma who had to leave this world too soon. Definitely larger than all of our aches and wants and petty insecurities.

"Keep watching, hon. It's coming." Dad's words felt like love. Now I understood why this was so important to him. We all needed this right now.

I looked at the empty chair next to him, and felt an unstoppable pull to be the one sitting in it. He didn't deserve to be sitting alone. Even with mom gone, we were still a family.

I leaned to Joss and whispered, "I need to go be with my dad."

He nodded, and when I got up to move, he reached out his hand. "Here, take this."

A key. The one from *Grandma's Attic*. I looked at him in awe.

"How did ...?"

"I saw you. Before you saw me. It seemed like you were looking for something in there."

I turned the key in my hand and shook my head in disbelief. "Weren't you looking for something too?"

He pulled a photo from his pocket and waved it at me. The one of the young woman with the glint in her eye. "I found it," he said, squeezing it tight between his fingers, then looking up to the sky.

I joined my dad, who to my amazement had opted to set his telescope camera to a timer, trusting its clicks to capture the memories. As I scooted in closer, he pulled his gaze from the eclipse just long enough for me to see the corner of his eyes crinkle up from behind his glasses. And in that moment, I knew we would make it through.

The sliver got smaller and smaller. And the darkness came in a thicker ink, quickly, until the last bit of the sun went completely out.

From all of our silence rose a collective gasp in the square. The black ball that was just our sun was now surrounded in an ethereal circle of purple and white.

Dad whispered with excitement, "Take your glasses off. You don't need them now, it's safe! Look!"

Out of the corner of my eye, I saw Joss take off his glasses. This was a moment none of us would have again for years—maybe our entire lives. Something that we couldn't share with anyone other than ourselves.

I thought of his grandma. And I thought of my mom. And I thought of my dad as I slid my hand into his, lowered my glasses, and looked to the sky.

Totality.

Contributors:

Cover Artist:

Patti Sullivan's abstract paintings and collages have been displayed in group and individual shows and in print in ARTLIFE mail art journal, Lummox, Evening Street Review, Spectrum, Café Solo among others. She branched out into poetry writing in the early 2000's. She has three poetry chapbooks, For The Day, DeerTree Press, Not Fade Away, Finishing Line Press and she won the Helen Kay Prize from Evening Street Press, for her chapbook, At The Booth Memorial Home for Unwed Mothers 1966. She became an editor with Evening Street Press later on. Individual poems have found homes in several journals including Chiron Review, Spillway, Cloudbank, Miramar, Hummingbird, Salt and most recently the online anthology Big Enough For Words, poets writing in response to photos in the Santa Barbara Library archives, Gunpowder Press.

About the painting *Ocean View*: I wanted to create the illusion of looking out a large window onto a view of the ocean, which I longed for! This was the largest canvas I had tackled since high school when my dad let me have an old piece of plywood out of the garage. I created a splatter paint mess which won first prize in a "Junk Art" contest in my class! Since then, I've never turned down any found objects to use in collages, sought out the broken and cast-off pieces of interesting items. In *Ocean View*, I wanted to create the idea of how the shells and debris mix together and swirl around also to use up my own discarded pieces of previous paintings.

M. Ait Ali was born in Agadir, Morocco. He attended the Higher School of Technology-Agadir and is currently pursuing a bachelor's degree in English. His work can be found in The *Tipton Poetry Journal, Variant Literature Inc.,*

Straylight Literary Arts Mag, Sandstorm UTPB Mag, and many other publications.

Connor Beeman is a recent graduate of Ohio University with a degree in Creative Writing & Women's, Gender, and Sexuality Studies. Much of his current work centers on the connections of place, deindustrialization, and queerness in his hometown of Akron and the greater Rust Belt. Previous publications include *The Oakland Arts Review, Polaris,* and Ohio University's own *Sphere*.

Julie Benesh has published stories, poems, and essays in *Tin House, Crab Orchard Review, Florida Review, Hobart, Cleaver* and many other places. She is a graduate of the MFA Program for Writers at Warren Wilson College in Writing and the recipient of an Illinois Arts Council Grant. Read more at juliebenesh.com.

Laurel Benjamin has work forthcoming or published in *Lily Poetry Review, South Florida Poetry Journal, Turning a Train of Thought Upside Down: An Anthology of Women's Poetry, Trouvaille Review, California Quarterly, The Midway Review, MacQueens Quinterly,* and more. Affiliated with the Bay Area Women's Poetry Salon and the Port Townsend Writers, she holds an MFA from Mills College and lives in the San Francisco Bay Area. More of her work can be found at https://thebadgerpress.blogspot.com

Princess Berry is from Piscataway, New Jersey. She has a bachelor's degree in English, creative writing with minors in History and Professional Writing. Besides being an editor and a teacher, she is also a full-time nerd who loves video games, books, writing and anime.

Coleman Bomar is a sleepless student who currently resides in Middle Tennessee. He counts his OCD as an advantage. His works have been featured by and/or are forthcoming in *Blink-Ink, SOFTBLOW, Eunoia Review, Moonpark Review, Maudlin House,* and many more. His work is soon to be archived at Yale's Beinecke Library.

Nico Bryan (she/her) is a queer hot girl poet from sun-shiny Florida. You can find her work in *Burrow Press Review* and beyond. You can find proof that she is, in fact, a hot girl, on Instagram at @nicobryo.

Tal Corvus is a queer Black writer, teacher, learner, farmer, and physical therapist. She grew up on a tether between the midwest and the southwest but now resides in the pacific northwest with her family, an assortment of animals, and many plants. Her writing explores the practices of perceiving and inhabiting physical and non-physical space. She has work forthcoming in *Foglifter*.

Kaliyah Dorsey is a senior at the University of Pennsylvania from New Jersey. Her fiction work has been published in *New Square*. You can find her @kaliyahdrsy on Twitter and IG.

Kris Faatz's short fiction has appeared or is forthcoming in journals including *Baltimore Review, Streetlight Magazine,* and *Typehouse,* and has received recognition in various contests, most recently making the shortlist for Philadelphia Stories's 2021 Marguerite McGlinn Fiction Prize and Fractured Literary's 2021 flash fiction prize. Her first novel, *To Love a Stranger* (Blue Moon Publishers, 2017), was a finalist for the 2016 Schaffner Press Music in Literature Award. Her second novel, *Fourteen Stones,* is forthcoming in 2022 from The Patchwork Raven (Wellington, NZ). Kris lives in Maryland, where she teaches creative writing and is a performing musician. Visit her online at krisfaatz.com.

B J Fischer is a writer living in Toledo, Ohio. He has published stories in *The Write Launch, the San Antonio Review, Artist's Studio, PIF Magazine, The View From Here, the Linden Avenue Literary Journal,* and *Blue Lake Review*. His essays have appeared in *The Fiddleback, Ardor, The (Toledo) Blade, the Bygone Bureau, Punchnel's, Thought Catalog, Impose Magazine, the Minneapolis Review of Baseball, midmajority.com,* and *Ontologica*.

D. B. Gardner, a graduate of Michigan State University, has previously appeared in *Flumes Literary Journal* and *East by Northeast Literary Magazine* and is currently working on a collection of short stories.

Robin Gow is a trans poet and young adult author from rural Pennsylvania. They are the author of *Our Lady of Perpetual Degeneracy* (Tolsun Books 2020) and the chapbook *Honeysuckle* (Finishing Line Press 2019). Their first young adult novel, *A Million Quiet Revolutions* is forthcoming March 2022 with FSG Books for Young Readers and their first essay collection *Blue Blood*, is forthcoming with the Nasiona Publishing House. Gow is a managing editor at *The Nasiona* and the assistant editor at large at Doubleback Books. They live in Allentown Pennsylvania and work at Bradbury-Sullivan LGBT Community Center.

Derek Graf is the author of *Green Burial*, winner of the 2021 Elixir Press Antivenom Poetry Award. His poems have appeared in *Portland Review, The Journal, The Boiler,* and elsewhere. He lives in New York City.

David C. Hall was born in Wisconsin and grew up in the suburbs of Chicago. He has lived in Spain since the 1970s, working as a teacher and translator, and has published novels and short stories in both Spanish and English. His novel *Barcelona Skyline* won the City of Getafe Crime Novel Prize in 2011. In 2017, he was awarded the José M. Valverde Prize for a short selection of poems in Spanish. More recently, and in English, he has published poems in *Driftwood Press, Columbia Poetry Review, The New Guard, Into the Void,* and *Crannóg.* He lives on the Mediterranean coast not far from Barcelona with his wife, a Beagle, and two cats.

Matt L. Hall (he/him) is a freelance journalist, author, and MFA student in creative writing at the University of Massachusetts Boston. Recently, Matt received the Chet Frederick Prize for excellence in fiction. Matt's stories have appeared in *pacificREVIEW*, and *The Ice Colony,* and his poetry has been featured in *The Watermark Journal.* He lives in Boston with his wife, two dogs, and two cats.

Jean Harper lives and writes in the rural Midwest. Her work has appeared in *The Florida Review, North American Review, Iowa Review,* and elsewhere. She has received fellowships from the National Endowment for the Arts, the Indiana Arts Commission, and been in residence at Yaddo, MacDowell, the Virginia Center for the Creative Arts, and the New Bedford Whaling Museum.

J.B. Hill is a Latina writer and native Texan. Her recent poetry and short stories have been published, and are forthcoming, in the *San Antonio Review, Beyond Words Literary Magazine, The Dillydoun Review, Coastal Shelf Literary Journal, Funicular Magazine, Bridge Eight Literary Magazine, Cathexis Northwest Press, The Closed Eye Open,* and *Wild Roof Journal.* She earned a BFA in Writing, Literature, and Publishing from Emerson College where she worked in the editorial department at Ploughshares. Hill has worked as a reporter in Boston, a screenplay analyst in Los Angeles, and a freelance writer and editor in Austin. You can find her on Instagram and Twitter @ideamakerupper and on

Facebook @jbhillwriter. Visit her website at
www.ideamakerupper. pcom.

Rachael Inciarte (she/they) lives in California. They hold an
MFA from Emerson College, with work nominated for the
Best of the Net and appearing in *Poetry Northwest, Spillway,
Normal School* and others. *What Kind of Seed Made You* is
their first chapbook, forthcoming from Finishing Line Press.
They are growing a garden and it is thriving.

Paris Jessie (she/her) is a black, queer poet/writer and
budding creative. She is a moon enthusiast rooted in deep
emotion. When not writing she is maybe dancing, dabbling
with music, or cuddling with grass. Find more at
iamparisjessie.com.

Bryana Joy is a writer, poet, and painter who works full-time
sending illustrated snail mail letters all over the world. She
also mails monthly new poems to subscribers in a postal
poetry project called Puzzle Pieces. Her poetry has appeared
in over three dozen literary journals, and is forthcoming in
Midwest Quarterly, Delmarva Review, Sand Journal, and
others. She has lived in Turkey, East Texas, and England, and
currently resides in the Lehigh Valley in Eastern
Pennsylvania. Find her at www.bryanajoy.com or on Twitter
and Instagram at @_bryana_joy.

Lytey Kay is a Jamaican-American poet from South Florida.
She received a BA in English and Creative Writing from
Florida Atlantic University and was a participant in AWP's
Writer to Writer Mentorship, Bread Loaf Environmental
Conference 2021, and Tin House Summer Workshop 2021.
Her poetry has been published or is forthcoming in *Hayden's
Ferry Review, SWWIM, Coastlines Literary Magazine*, and
Saw Palm.

Laura Keller is a young adult fiction writer who lives in Kansas City. Her work has appeared in the Northern Colorado Writers anthology *Pooled Ink*, as well as *Young Adult Review Network*, for which she received an SCBWI Magazine Merit Award. Her YA fiction has also been recognized with awards from SouthWest Writers, League of Utah Writers, and Writer's Digest. When she's not writing, she loves to hang out with her family, play guitar, and teach reading to lively elementary students. Find Laura on Instagram: @laurakellerwrites.

Justin Lacour lives in New Orleans and edits *Trampoline: A Journal of Poetry*. His poetry has appeared in *New Orleans Review* (Web Features), *Parhelion, B O D Y*, and other journals.

Marsha Lewis lives outside Philadelphia, PA. She grows vegetables for a community center in the city and assists people with disabilities in finding creative ways to thrive during the pandemic. She likes writing down words and rearranging them. Her poems have appeared in *Panoply, Apricity, Red Weather,* and *Gyroscope*.

Gabrielle "Rie" Lee is a California-based writer and editor. She holds an MFA in Creative Writing from Eastern Washington University and her first book, *Comforts We Despise*, is forthcoming from Zoozil Media (direct to publisher). Her shorter works have been published in the likes of *DRYLAND, Switchback, Acentos Review*, and various anthologies, and she keeps a blog called Part of This Complete Breakfast. Find her on The Twitter @yesrielee.

Christopher Louvet lives in Hanoi, Vietnam. His work has appeared or is forthcoming in *Denver Quarterly, The Main Street Rag, The Dead Mule School of Southern Literature,*

Washington Square Review, the Greensboro Review, and online with *McSweeney's Internet Tendency*.

Letizia Mariani resides in Irvine, CA, where she is pursuing a PhD in English. Her work has appeared in *The Summit Avenue Review, ellipsis...literature and art,* and *Tint Journal,* and she was recipient of the 2017 Lon Otto Prize in Creative Writing.

Matthew S. Mayes is a recent graduate of the University of California, Santa Barbara where he studied Biopsychology. Currently, he is working as the clinical office manager of an outpatient psychiatric clinic, waiting to apply to medical school. His poetry has appeared in *Young Ravens Literary Review.*

Alex Mika is currently a graduate student at the University of Connecticut. He released his first chapbook, a mock field log and memoir called *Alex and the Dinosaur Prints*, in 2020. He enjoys writing poetry and drama, making music, and futilely trying to train his cat to do tricks.

Cindy Milwe is a writer and teacher who lives in Venice, CA. Her work has been published in many journals and magazines, including *5 AM, Alaska Quarterly Review, Poetry East, Poet Lore, The William and Mary Review, Flyway, Talking River Review,* and *The Georgetown Review*, among others. She also has poems in two anthologies: *Another City: Writing from Los Angeles* (City Lights, 2001) and *Changing Harm to Harmony: The Bullies and Bystanders Project* (Marin Poetry Center Press, 2015). Her poem "Hunger" was selected as First Prize Winner for the Myra Shapiro Poetry Contest, sponsored by The International Women's Writing Guild, and her poem "Legacy" was the first prize winner for the Parent/Writer Fellowship at Martha's Vineyard Institute of Creative Writing. This year, her poem "Memorial" was nominated for a Pushcart

Prize. Her first full-length collection, *Salvage*, will be published by Finishing Line Press in early 2022.

Sabyasachi Näg has published fiction and poetry. His work has appeared or forthcoming in *Anomaly, Canadian Literature, Grain, Meat for Tea Journal, The Antigonish Review, The Dalhousie Review, and The Windsor Review,* among others. He is an alumnus of the Community of Writers at Squaw, the Writer's Studio at Simon Fraser University, the Humber School for Writers, the BANFF Centre for Arts and is currently an MFA candidate in the Creative Writing program at the University of British Columbia. He was born in Calcutta, India, and lives with his wife in Mississauga, Ontario.

R.C. Neighbors is an Oklahoma expatriate who currently resides in the Rio Grande Valley where he serves as a Lecturer at the Texas A&M Higher Education Center. He received his Ph.D. in Creative Writing from Texas A&M University and his M.F.A from Hollins University. He lives with his wife, four kids, two dogs, two orphan kitties, and a photo of himself with the head of hair and motorcycle he used to have. His work has appeared in *Tampa Review, Barely South Review, Found Poetry Review, Southern Poetry Anthology: Texas,* and elsewhere.

Cassady O'Reilly-Hahn is a poet with an MA from Claremont Graduate University. He is a managing editor for *Foothill: A Poetry Journal* that highlights graduate student voices. He works for AudioEyes, a company that describes TV and film for blind viewers. In his free time, Cassady writes Haiku for his personal blog, orhawrites and his Instagram @cassady_orha. Cassady currently resides in Claremont, California, where he can be found flipping through fantasy novels in a cozy recliner on the weekends.

Olivia Piper is a Connecticut native, a poet, and works as both an Academic Coordinator and an English Instructor with multiple educational equity nonprofits. She has been published in *HerHeart Poetry, The Connecticut River Review*, and *Funicular Magazine*. More of her work can be found on her Instagram @sunflowerpoetryblog

JC Reilly is the author of the narrative poetry collection *What Magick May Not Alter* (Madville Publishing, 2020). She won the Sow's Ear Poetry Prize in 2020 for the forthcoming chapbook *Amo e Canto*, and she serves as the Managing Editor of *Atlanta Review*. Since the pandemic started, she has worn out all of her pajamas. Follow her @aishatonu.

Aurin Shaila Nusrat Sheyck is a poet and a PhD student based in the beautiful city of Ottawa, Ontario. Her work has appeared or is forthcoming in *Without a doubt* by *New York Quarterly, Cotyledon* by Vancouver Poetry House, in *THAT literary review, Reality Break Press*, etc. Her self-published poetry book, *Nostalgia or Sunset*, was published in 2017. Introspection, pacifism, mysticism, love for nature and being—these are the ideas she explores in her work wrapping them around relatable mundane pictures of daily lives. Her pieces accentuate the elements of extra-ordinary hopes, ambitions, and stories of ordinary people she observes in the metro, subways, or streets. Aurin is a bilingual poet and writes in English as well as in Bengali.

Kris Spencer has written seven books. He is a regular contributor to magazines in a journalistic career that spans over 20 years. His poems have been published in a number of journals across the continents. Most recently in *Briefly Write, Allegro, The Literary Bohemian, Acumen, Orchards Poetry Journal, Fenlands Poetry Journal,* and *The Balloon Literary Journal*. A Fellow of the Royal Geographical Society, a theme in his work is sense of place. Kris is a Headteacher living and working in West London. He is married and has two children. He was born and grew up in a village outside Bolton. Previously, he has studied, worked and lived in Hull, Cincinnati, Oxford, and the Bailiwick of Jersey.

Carole Symer is a practicing psychologist in Ann Arbor, Michigan, where she works with adolescents and young adults, from whom she learns the exquisite effort it takes to language a life. Symer also teaches at New York University and has authored nearly a thousand neuropsychological evaluations to help neurodiverse learners fulfill their civil and human rights fulfilled, and discover more pleasure in daily life. Her essays, articles, and poems have appeared in *Across the Margin, Michigan Chronicle, Mutha Magazine, Sky Island Journal, The Passed Note, Wild Roof Journal,* and elsewhere. She is the 2020 recipient of the Anne-Marie Ooman & Katey Schultz ICCA Creative Writing Scholarship. Her debut chapbook, *Glint,* is forthcoming in June 2021 from Small Harbor Publishing.

Durell Thompson is a student, teacher, father, husband, and son. Through his poetry he looks to explore the multifaceted connections that define the African American experience in the United States. Moreover, he uses his poetry as a way to embrace his roles as an educator, writer, and father, and to prepare his son to live and thrive as a black man. Works from Durell Thompson have appeared in *Bayou Magazine* ("Black Son"), *Beacon* (SHSU review) ("Welfare Line", "Bilingual Waitress", "Watermelon Lady", and "My view on Clouds (ode to "Darius and the Clouds")."

Emily Wagner has been writing poetry for enjoyment since her early teens. After earning a B.A. in English Writing and working for a community non-profit for a short stint, she went back to school and earned her teaching certification. Since 2005, she has been teaching all levels of high school English.

She has loved poetry since, as a young girl, she was introduced to Emily Dickinson, and since then she has tried to share the importance of poetry with her students. Her poetry has been featured in *The Dillydoun Review* and in *Wingless Dreamer* and is forthcoming in *Beyond Words Literary Magazine*. She lives in rural central Pennsylvania with her husband and two sons.

Michael Waterson is a retired journalist originally from Pittsburgh PA. His working career includes stints as a forest firefighter, San Francisco taxi driver, and wine educator. He earned a BA from San Francisco State and an MFA from Mills College. His poems have appeared in numerous online and print journals, including *California Quarterly, Cathexis Northwest* and *The Bookends Review*.

Tria Wen's writing has been published or is forthcoming in the *Washington Post, The Rumpus, Narratively, and Slant'd,* among other places. *Tin House, VONA*, and *Rooted & Written* alumna, she has won a CAC Emerging Artist Fellowship, Charles C. Dawe Innovation in Publishing Award, and SCWC BIPOC Writer Fellowship. She is a co-founding editor of the Black Allyship column at *Mochi Magazine*, co-creator of Make America Dinner Again, and has spoken on NPR, BBC, and at SXSW about her work. You can find her on Instagram @triawenwriting.

Thank you for reading! Stay in touch:

www.blackfoxlitmag.com
Website

www.facebook.com/blackfoxlit
Facebook

@blackfoxlit
Twitter & Instagram

www.blackfoxlitmag.com/contact/
Newsletter

Check out some of our previous issues:

Find more of our issues at blackfoxlitmag.com!

Resources for Writers from BFLM Editor Racquel Henry's Writer's Atelier:

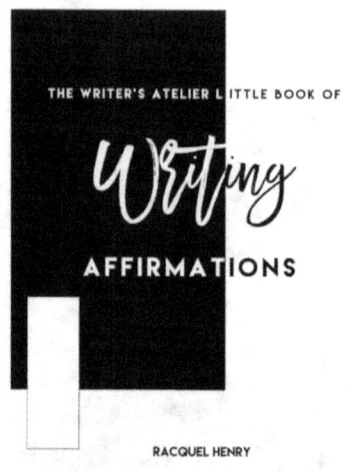

The Writer's Atelier Little Book of Writing Affirmations

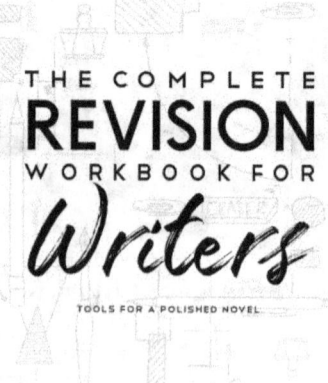

The Complete Revision Workbook for Writers